4

FREQUENT FLYER

By Kinky Friedman

Frequent Flyer
When the Cat's Away
A Case of Lone Star
Greenwich Killing Time

FREQUENT FLYER

KINKY FRIEDMAN

William Morrow and Company, Inc.
New York

Library of Congress Cataloging-in-Publication Data

Friedman, Kinky,
    Frequent Flyer / Kinky Friedman,
    p.   cm.
    ISBN 0-688-08166-5
    I. Title.
    PS3556.R527G736   1989
    813'.54—dc19   89-31012
                                                                     CIP

Printed in the United States of America

First Edition

1   2   3   4   5   6   7   8   9   10

BOOK DESIGN BY JAYE ZIMET

The tattooed lady left the circus train,
Lost all of her pictures in the rain,
I wonder if you're happy, I wonder if you're free,
I wonder if you'll ever know the mark you left on me.

I'm the Wild Man from Borneo
The Wild Man from Bornco
You come to see what you want to see
You come to see but you never come to know.

1

▲▲▲

It was flyover country.

Flyover country, of course, is what New Yorkers call any place between New York and Los Angeles.

I was standing in a snow-covered cemetery somewhere outside Cleveland, Ohio, and the bagpipe player they'd hired for the funeral was wearing long johns under his kilt. It was so cold the teardrops were turning to sleet before they hit the ground.

I'd gotten the phone call the afternoon before. I'd been dozing at the desk in my loft in the Village. It was a stranger's voice, saying, "You were a friend of John Morgan's, weren't you?" One of those rather awkward, unsettling moments in life just before the past tense hits you like the *Sunset Limited.*

"Yeah," I said, struggling to regain my spiritual balance.

"John died yesterday in Columbus."

The voice paused, and I lighted a cigar just for something to do.

"He often talked about when the two of you were together in the Peace Corps. In the jungles of Borneo, wasn't it?"

"Yeah." I could see the shimmering laughter in John Morgan's eyes. They were the color of banana trees on the other side of a dream.

"The funeral's tomorrow in Cleveland," the voice said. "Do you think you can make it?"

"Yeah," I said.

The guy gave me the time and place of the funeral, and I wrote it down. He told me his name, but by the time I'd cradled the blower I'd already forgotten. If he'd said his name was Zippy the Pinhead, I doubt if it would've blown my skirt up too much. You half listen to those kinds of phone calls. Part of you hears the voice on the other end of the line and part of you strains to hear that faraway sort of music Van Gogh might've composed if he'd poked out his eyes instead of cutting off his ear.

I listened to the music for a while. Then I lost it to the growling of the garbage trucks out on Vandam Street.

I called Kelly, my friendly travel agent, and told her I was going on a trip.

"Is it business or pleasure?" she asked.

"I'm going to Cleveland," I said.

So here I was in the bone orchard. My thoughts skittered crazily like the snowflakes, and like the snowflakes, crashed in silent finality against cold marble stone.

The priest had said a few *cosa nostras*, and the bagpipe player was bravely squeaking and farting his way through a lilting Irish tune in 15-degree weather at a funeral for somebody he probably didn't know. Bagpipe players don't get a lot of work these days. When a gig comes along, they take it.

If it'd been a wedding I'd probably have tried to stop it. But it wasn't a wedding. It was a funeral. The only funeral you've got a right to try to stop is your own, and that's a full-time job.

I hadn't seen John in maybe five years and had only gotten together with him on four or five occasions in the almost twenty years since I'd been back in the States. I didn't feel too bad about it though. The only way to keep a good friendship going these days is to stay the hell away from people.

Yet when you've lived two years in the jungle with someone, you get to know him pretty well, and when the unctuous undertaker had taken me to the open casket that morning, I knew something was wrong.

I glanced across at John's parents. Subtract twenty years and they looked just like the people in the photograph that John had shown me in Borneo. I gazed around at the rest of the family and friends standing by the casket near the gaping hole in the ground. The grief on their faces seemed deep and genuine.

I was confused, but I didn't think it was the time or place to raise my hand and ask for a point of clarification. I kept my thoughts to myself as I grimly watched them lower the casket into the frozen ground. Five years can change somebody, I thought. But never that much. No, I wasn't imagining things.

I couldn't stop the funeral. And there was something else I couldn't stop. I couldn't stop wondering.

Why was the body they were burying *not* John Morgan?

They didn't show a movie on the flight from Cleveland back to New York. They didn't have to. In my head a double feature was going on, and by the time we got to LaGuardia it had pretty well twisted itself into a sick, synaptic pretzel of *Lord Jim* and *Invasion of the Body Snatchers*. They didn't show a cartoon, either. That was coming later, but I didn't know it.

At LaGuardia I grabbed a hack driven by a non-English–speaking Third World gentleman named Hassan. He only spoke enough English, it emerged, to tell me to put out my cigar. I, of course, not wishing to bring additional grief to the Third World, grudgingly obliged.

"The last good Arab," I muttered as I killed the cigar, "was probably Muhammad." I don't know whether Hassan understood, but he made several glottal noises, and off we roared onto the Parkway.

I sat back to enjoy the ride. After visiting America for a while, it's always nice to get back to New York.

Hassan had not heard of things like Greenwich Village or the George Washington Bridge, and he did not take kindly to the news that I was a big admirer of the great Islamic poet Danny Thomas. By the time we got to 199B Vandam, a hard frost had settled both outside and inside the cab. I gave Hassan a tip commensurate with the service. He gave me an unpleasant Middle Eastern sign with his hand as he drove away.

The freight elevator with the one exposed light bulb was in use, so I legged it with the suitcase up four dank flights of stairs. On three, I had to kick a tricycle out of the way and an empty bottle of Early Times. Kid was sloppy, but he had good taste in whiskey.

I unlocked the door to my loft. It smelled like a big cigar had died there. Maybe a small side order of cat shit. It was a lot like love. Sometimes you had to go away before you noticed it. It was about 27 degrees Fahrenheit. Colder than an eccentric old lady's bosom. I went over to the radiator to turn it on, but it was already on. It put out about as well as some broads I've known. At least it didn't want to sit down and have a good talk.

As I walked over to the desk, I noticed a fairly recent cat turd lying equidistant between my two red telephones. Both phones were connected to the same line, sort of to enhance the importance of my incoming wounded. Of course, it wasn't going to be too pleasant answering either one of them with a feline souvenir lying there right in the middle.

Cats often present you with things. Sometimes it's a bird; sometimes it's a turd. This one didn't have any wings.

I was staring at the cat turd, which was shaped vaguely like Nicaragua, when the phones rang. Gingerly, I picked up the blower on the left.

"Start talkin'," I said.

"Are you Kinky?" It was the husky, foreign-flavored voice of a young woman.

"Who wants to know?"

"My name is Carmen," she said. "I am John Morgan's fiancée."

Don't be too sure, I thought.

"Something has happened," she said. "I must come to see you." I felt myself shiver suddenly from the chill in the room.

"Fine," I said. "Where are you calling from?"

"A place where people disappear," she said.

3

I removed the cat turd, but it didn't seem to clear the air very much. Here I was back from Cleveland, and I still hadn't buried John Morgan. Was it possible that out of three hundred or more people at the funeral, I was the only one who recognized that there'd been one minor problem?

▲ 12

I walked over to the kitchen and opened the window. I looked at New York. A cold storage warehouse. A couple of rusty fire escapes. A billboard with an aircraft flying away to somewhere else. Nice view.

But you can't really see New York the way you can see San Francisco or San Diego or Dallas. New York is like a lady standing in the fog. From one angle she looks like a beautiful young girl. From another, she's a weatherbeaten old whore.

In New York you've got to know all the angles.

There are more people, pigeons, and potholes in New York than cross-ties on the railroad or stars in the skies, and there's no elbow room for Daniel Boone. But people in this city have something else. They all feel that it means something just to be here. For example, a mugger in New York knows that he's at the top of his profession. Child molesters, hit men, killer fags, all smile a secret little smile to themselves in New York. They know they are the best that they can be.

From my kitchen window I could see a bench on the corner with a black man and an old white woman sitting on opposite ends. They each appeared to be talking to themselves. Nothing wrong with that. I've talked to myself for years. They say it's when you start answering yourself that you've got problems. I didn't have to worry about that. Tonight I didn't have any answers. I closed the window.

It was a Friday night in the dreary middle of a frigid February. The time was moving inexorably toward eight o'clock, the peak time for millions of people to start actively seeking fun. I was not one of these people. I let fun come to me.

I had promised my friend McGovern earlier in the week that I'd drop by his place this evening. McGovern was a large half-Indian, half-Irish reporter for the *Daily News* who had been grudgingly invaluable to me on several occasions in the past. I didn't see how he could help me now, but you never knew.

If nothing else, tonight McGovern was cooking my favorite: Chicken McGovern.

I put on my hat and coat, grabbed a few cigars for the road, and headed for the door. The cat was still hiding someplace, but that didn't bother me. One less person to say good-bye to.

"That couch," said McGovern, nodding toward the couch I was sitting on, "has been across the Atlantic twice." It was a pink velvet affair, and it took up about half of his quaint, newspaper-strewn apartment. McGovern paused to take a long drink from a tall glass.

"Fascinating," I said. "When's the Chicken McGovern going to be ready?" The aroma reminded me of curries in the Far East. And of other things. There had to be a mistake somewhere. . . .

"It once belonged to Dermot Purgavie," McGovern was saying, "the noted columnist for the *London Daily Mail,* who took it aboard the *Queen Elizabeth II* along with his first wife . . ."

I'd never known John to wear a beard, and yet the corpse had had a beard. But still, I thought, I would've recognized my old friend. . . .

". . . from New York to a Victorian sitting room in Hampstead, London. After a while, the first wife decided she didn't much like the couch—or Dermot, for that matter. . . ."

. . . Either I was letting my imagination run away

with me, or something very peculiar indeed was going on. . . .

". . . So Dermot took the couch and himself from the Victorian sitting room, traveled across with it again on the _QE2_ . . ."

. . . If I wasn't careful, I thought, I was going to need a couch and a shrink to go with it. . . .

". . . and stored it in a warehouse in New Jersey. Are you with me so far?"

"I'm afraid so," I said.

"Then fire struck the warehouse in New Jersey."

"What an interesting story."

"But it doesn't end there."

"No, of course not."

"The couch was declared legally dead. Dermot collected five grand in insurance. The second wife didn't like it any better than the first. And Dermot gave me the couch."

"Generous," I said. If John Morgan was legally dead, I thought, and he wasn't the same guy I'd known in Borneo, then where—

"I seem to remember a certain down-and-out country singer who didn't mind crashing on it from time to time. Not to mention Tom Baker, Frederick Exley, Vaughn Meader, and the great Australian journalist Piers Akerman."

Piers had told me that one night while he was sleeping on McGovern's couch, the gracious host had sat on him, thereby causing grievous injury to his scrotum. But there was no point in bringing that up now; the Chicken McGovern was almost ready. I never discussed religion, or politics, or McGovern anecdotes while eating Chicken McGovern. It gave one gas.

So, as we knocked off the Chicken McGovern, which was killer bee, I told McGovern all about my trip to Cleveland.

"When I get to the paper in the morning," said McGovern, "I'll see if I can find him in the morgue." He laughed his hearty Irish laugh. "No pun intended."

Walking home in the cold that night, I began to feel like Kafka's character in *The Trial*, raked by situations and circumstances that seemed unreal, far away, and beyond my control or comprehension. It was an uncomfortable, almost frightening feeling.

As I rode up to my loft in the freight elevator, I began to wonder if I wasn't really losing my mind. Like the security guard on the Texas Tower said about the mild-mannered Charles Whitman after he'd suddenly climbed the tower and shot twenty-six people, "It'll happen to you."

When I walked into the loft, the cat was sitting on the kitchen table waiting for me. Her eyes narrowed slightly and went from green to yellow like a sentient traffic light. It was enough to make the hairs on the back of your neck come to full attention. The cat always translated my innermost fears with uncanny accuracy. This time there was no mistaking it. Something was as wrong as acid rain.

I fed the cat some tuna. I thought about emptying the litter box. I walked into the bathroom and peered into the rain-room, where I kept the litter box. With only one unfortunate exception—a morning some time ago when I'd been on the third ring of Saturn—I always took it out before taking a shower. Just a homemaker's tip.

The litter box didn't look too good. Neither did the rest of the world. I decided to let them both be. I was always a little hesitant to empty the litter box these days after my friend Ratso, the editor of *National Lampoon,* in his clever, Watson-like way, had hidden over a quarter of a million dollars of top-quality cocaine in it almost a year ago.

I was the one he was hiding it from, of course.

The results had been very unpleasant.

But I had to admit, however, that, with the exception of the litter-box incident, Ratso had been very helpful with my forays into crime-solving.

I looked in the litter box again. It was good for another few weeks at least. That was more than I could say with any certainty about myself.

I walked back into the living room and thought about John Morgan. It's funny how even a short period of time can create doubts in your mind. Can fade an impression that once you were so sure about. I didn't know what to think.

I poured out a double shot of snake piss into my old bull's horn shot glass and carried it over to the desk. There were a few things I could do, I thought. I could set a fire under McGovern's large Irish buttocks and at least obtain in short order Morgan's obit in the Cleveland papers. Christ, computers were wonderful. I could sit on my own buttocks and wait for the mysterious Carmen broad to reestablish commo. I could call a few old Peace Corps buddies of mine who'd also known John in Borneo and see if they'd heard anything about either his recent demise or to the contrary.

I made a few calls. One to Dylan Ferrero in Texas and one to Joe Hollis in North Carolina. Nobody home twice.

I got up and knocked a few cobwebs off the old stereo. I put on a cassette Ratso had given me. Chinese children singing Christmas carols. Because of my years on the road as a country singer, I had come to hate the sound of the human voice singing. At least with this cassette, I didn't have to understand the words.

I went back to the desk, killed about half the shot, took a cigar out of my porcelain Sherlock Holmes head and set fire to it, always keeping the tip of the cigar well above the flame. I sat back in the chair, put my feet up on the desk, killed the rest of the shot, and listened to the Chinese version of "Silver Bells."

Friday night in the Big Apple.

It was a coffee-colored river. I could see it clearly as I sat at my desk that night, many shots and many Chinese Christmas carols later. It seemed to flow out of a childhood storybook, peaceful and familiar, continue its sluggish way beneath the tropical sun, and then, at some point that you could never quite see, pick up force and become that opaque uncontrollable thing roaring in your ears, blinding your eyes, rushing relentlessly round the bends of understanding, beyond the banks of imagination.

One of the comforting things about the Borneo jungle, or the *ulu*, as it's called, is that it is fairly immutable. Although evangelical missionaries with third-grade educations portray Jesus as a bogeyman and teach the natives to throw away their beads, cut their hair, and sing "Oh, Susanna," progress, as we like to call it, is slow. As the Kayan tribesmen tell you when they say good-bye: *"Pleheigh, pleheigh, tuan,"* which roughly translated means, "Slowly, slowly, lord."

The Kayans, former headhunters, are a beautiful, gentle

people. They wear their hair in sort of an early Beatles' style, as they have for hundreds of years. Tattoos are popular with the men, and the women wear heavy earrings that eventually stretch their earlobes down almost to their breasts.

Kayan men often drill holes in the heads of their penises and insert a length of bone with feathers on each end. This is called a *palang,* and was probably the grandfather of the French tickler. Unfortunately, hemorrhaging often resulted in the female, and the *palang*'s popularity has declined somewhat. My friend Joe Hollis always wanted a *palang,* but in the end, quite to everyone's disappointment, he settled for a tattoo.

In the West, you never know what's going to happen from day to day. When you wake up in the morning, you've got to wait for Bryant Gumbel to tell you if it's safe to go outside and then you've got to wait for Willard Scott to tell you what to wear. But somehow I was pretty sure Borneo was still as I remembered. Of course, there was no way to really know. Maybe now I was looking at things with different eyes. Twenty years can change a dreamer far more than they can a river.

I closed my eyes and could see John Morgan and me in a small boat in the gathering darkness. We must have been four or five days, as near as I could recall, upriver from Long Lama, the little village we were both based out of. John had told me he'd been working on some kind of community health project in this area. I'd never been this far into the *ulu* before. The trees along the banks of the river looked tall, strange, and vaguely ominous.

"Durian trees," John said. "The fruits are encased in a hard, spiked shell, and every so often they fall on somebody's head and kill 'em."

"That's good to know."

Morgan smiled mischievously. "Also," he said, "if you

eat durian at the same time as you drink *tuak*, the native wine, you'll die."

"Yeah," I said, "but I bet it's a hell of a way to go."

"Better than having your head lopped off with a *parang* and put in a basket to decorate the *ruai* in somebody's longhouse."

"C'mon," I said. "They don't do that anymore." John smiled devilishly, and I could see what he'd looked like as a little kid.

"Did Hitler shave his moustache?" he asked.

The trees became invisible, and the sky and water joined together. John had maintained that we were near a longhouse, and I hoped to hell he was right. You don't know what dark is until you've been in the *ulu* at night. There were legends about ghosts, or *hantus*, as the Kayans called them. There was black magic that had been practiced diligently for generations. There were stories of witches who flew, using their ears for wings. The dark night of the *ulu* was closing in palpably around us. It was almost enough to make you want to throw away your beads and sing "Oh, Susanna."

After we'd drifted with nothing but a flashlight and a kerosene lamp for a lot longer than I would've liked, we saw lights ahead of us flickering on the river. Soon we could make out men rowing small carved wooden *prahus* and carrying torches.

"What the hell is it?" I asked. "A war party?"

John laughed. "More like a fishing party." His eyes twinkled and, as usual, told more than his words.

We watched the silent torches for a moment gliding slowly toward us on the river in the night. "Because of the current," John said, "and because they get *mabbok* on the *tuak*, they never do catch many fish. In fact, their word for fishing translates into English to mean 'visiting the fish.'"

I could see John's face in the lamplight—young, un-

lined, gentle as the spirit of the Kayan people. On that coffee-colored river, at that time, I felt very close to him
"Visiting the fish," I said. "I like that."
"It's yours," he said.

Saturday morning I nursed a very unpleasant, almost cloying hangover, and listened to McGovern recite John Morgan's obituary from the *Cleveland Plain Dealer*. Hell of a way to start the weekend.

"Not a bad obit, as they go," McGovern said brightly. 'Maybe a little bit stiff." McGovern laughed loudly, and my hangover hung over all the way to my left eyeball.

"That's cute, McGovern. Very sensitive to take advantage of a friend in his time of grief."

"Grief?" shouted McGovern. "You already said you're not even sure who it was that you buried! The way I see it, you only have two courses of action."

There was a third course of action, and that was to hang up the phone, but the obit had been so sketchy and unforthcoming that I found myself hopelessly holding on to the blower as if it were a lifeline from the *Lusitania*. About the only thing the obit had confirmed was that Morgan had been in the Peace Corps in South America. Either that was a factual error, or John had really been in the Peace Corps in South America before he'd been assigned to Borneo. An unusual reassignment, but not unheard of. I'd have to check it out.

"The two courses of action being . . .?" I asked rather testily. I was starting to feel kind of dizzy.

"They should be obvious," said McGovern.

"If they were obvious, I wouldn't be talking to a large, cheerful mick at nine o'clock in the morning. What the hell are they?"

"Get an exhumation order," McGovern said, "or, as you always say, get a checkup from the neck up."

I followed the third course of action and cradled the blower.

Still irritated with McGovern and half in a throbbing fog, I stoked up the espresso machine, fed the cat, and banged around the kitchen looking for my IMUS IN THE MORNING coffee mug. Apparently, someone had stolen it.

"The theft must've occurred while I was in Cleveland," I muttered bitterly to the cat. The cat was eating and didn't like to be interrupted. She didn't respond.

I found a chipped but suitable replacement mug, loaded it with thick, steaming espresso, and took it over to my desk. I took a few tentative slurps, fired up a half-smoked cigar I found in the wastebasket, and pondered the mysterious occurrences that had intruded upon my life within the past forty-eight hours.

First there was the bewildering situation in Cleveland, beginning with the phone call about Morgan's death and ending with a large number of normal-looking Americans burying a body that I was almost certain did not belong to John Morgan.

Then had come the phone call from someone who had said that her name was Carmen, that she'd been a friend of John Morgan's and that she was calling from a place where people disappear. I remembered, at the time of the call, feeling a sudden chill. Now, in the pale light of Saturday morning, I felt myself shudder again. I took a healthy slug of the espresso and puffed a couple times on the cigar to clear my head.

Normally, this would've been enough to fill anybody's plate for a while, but then I'd had to hear McGovern's tedious dissertation about the history of his couch, walk twenty blocks through a dismal, specter-ridden night wondering openly about my sanity, and get home just in time to see the cat's eyes change colors.

I wondered if there was a support group for this kind of situation. If there was, I didn't think I wanted to belong.

Add to all this the disappearance of my favorite coffee mug, and you could see what a fragile state my mind was in. Any shrink will tell you that people who are already under great mental stress and then happen to lose their IMUS IN THE MORNING coffee mugs are only a Texas two-step away from becoming Jesus or Napoleon impersonators.

I was too tall for Napoleon and too o-l-d for Jesus.

Maybe they had somebody else.

The only person I could think of who had known John Morgan as well as I had was Dylan Ferrero. I'd met Dylan in Borneo, and when we'd got back to the States, he'd become the road manager for my band, the Texas Jewboys. After the Jewboys had gone on sabbatical, he'd traded in his sunglasses and python jacket for a coat and tie, gotten married, settled down, and become a schoolteacher. Nothing wrong with that. Might've done it myself, but I never could find the right tie.

"Dylan," I said, "I think I have some bad news."

" 'Bad news travels like wildfire; good news travels slow.' " Dylan was fond of quoting lyrics from rock 'n' roll songs, a trait that sometimes irritated me, but he had so many good traits and I had so many repellent ones that I usually let it slide.

I told Dylan what had happened in Cleveland. Unlike myself, he was a good listener, and absorbed it all in shocked silence.

Then he said, "Well, Jesus Christ, hoss, why don't you call his parents and find out?"

"Dylan, it was an open-casket funeral."

"Shit," he said. "I haven't seen Morgan in some years, but the last I'd heard he was back in the Far East. He seemed to hop back and forth pretty often. I just don't believe he's dead. It's kind of like 'something's happenin' and you don't know what it is, do you, Mr. Jones?' "

"Dylan," I said irritably, "were there any strange incidents in Borneo involving John that you can remember?"

"Well, there was the time Morgan brought a tribal medicine man over to Hollis's house one morning to give him a *palang* operation. That was pretty unusual. Hollis had gone fairly native at the time, but he woosied out at the last minute."

"That's understandable," I said.

"I guess he figured a bone in the nose was one thing, but a bone in the hose was quite another."

"Quite," I said. "Look, if you think of anything besides the *palang* incident, call me."

" 'If my memory serves me well,' " he said, "but it was 'long ago and far away.' "

When I hung up with Dylan, I found myself thinking about John Morgan and smiling wistfully.

9

"That Carmen person sounds interesting," said Ratso as he put a piece of pork approximately the size and shape of a golf ball into his mouth with a pair of chopsticks. I'd told him the whole story. It was pushing eleven o'clock and we were having dim sum at the Golden Palace on Mott Street. Ratso pronounced the name "Carmen" like "common."

"What kind of accent did you say she had?" he asked. He picked up a piece of shrimp that appeared to be covered with a clear layer of mucous membrane.

"Foreign," I said.

"That doesn't help much. By your standards, anybody who doesn't say 'Thank ye. Y'all have a nice day now' has a foreign accent."

"I'm not quite that parochial, Ratso. In fact, her accent sounded a lot more pleasant than yours. She sounded kind of like an upscale Mexican." I helped myself to some tripe in black bean sauce.

All around us four generations of Chinese were chatting mysteriously to each other. Their words seemed to cascade off the ceiling of the big room and flit together like little Oriental birds. Ratso caught me listening and paused to listen himself.

"Sounds nice—almost like music—doesn't it?" he said. "I wonder what they're all saying."

"They're probably all saying, 'Thank ye. Y'all have a nice day now,' " I said. I took out a cigar and began a little preinflammatory foreplay. I poured us both another cup of hot Chinese tea.

"You know," said Ratso, "that 'place where people disappear' business seems to ring a bell. Have you given it any thought?"

"Oh, a nightmare or two. I figure she's either calling from the Bermuda Triangle or from the transporter room of the starship *Enterprise.*"

"Let me think about it for a while," said Ratso in his most Watson-like manner. "A place where people disappear . . ."

"Take all the time you want," I said. "We're not going to bring back the dead."

"*If* he's dead," said Ratso.

Later, while walking west on Canal Street, we passed a large flock of flea markets, which put Ratso on cloud eight and a half and bored me right through the pavement. I started to drag Ratso away, but I saw a little flame in his eyes that burned with the spirit of a woman window-shopping at Tiffany, so I went along with him relatively good-naturedly. After all, practically his whole wardrobe came from this kind of place. This was Ratso's Fifth Avenue. Ratso's Savile Row.

By the time we got to Soho, the weather was thawing out a bit. It was almost warm enough to dodge tourists. We were passing a very trendy new store that sold only used dashikis when Ratso grabbed my arm.

"This Carmen person, if she exists—"

"Of course she exists," I said. "She called me."

"Of course," Ratso said, looking at me peculiarly.

There was an uncomfortable silence during which time Ratso let go of my arm and said, "Ever heard of the *desaparecidos?*"

"Sure," I said. "It's the new Mexican restaurant on the Upper East Side."

Ratso laughed rather indulgently. "No, Kinkster, I'm afraid not," he said. "The *desaparecidos* are a group of people—many thousands of them—whose views ran counter to certain governments in Latin America. Beginning in the late sixties, this whole group of people seems to have, quite literally, disappeared. Even their own families have no earthly idea where they are."

I stared at Ratso for a moment. "Watson," I said, "you always cease to amaze me. But how does all this tie in with John Morgan?"

Ratso had a very troubled look in his eye. It was one part sadness, one part doubt, and if I didn't know better, I would've said it was one part pity.

"He was—or is—your friend," said Ratso gently. "You tell me."

Carmen didn't call. Blower traffic in general was pretty light. That left a hell of a lot of quality time that weekend for me and the cat.

In the loft above us Winnie Katz's lesbian dance class thudded away at unexpected intervals throughout the weekend. Whenever the thudding ceased, it seemed to be picked up in a growling refrain from the Greek chorus of garbage trucks out on Vandam Street. All in all, it was a peaceful time, quite conducive to self-reflection. Self-reflection, of course, is when you put a slice of your life under the microscope, focus it in, and observe it carefully. Then you stand back and try to avoid projectile vomit.

It was sometime over the weekend that I decided I

might like to have an affair with Winnie. She was demurely attractive and quite character-laden, and she reminded me of a kleptomaniac I'd once seen briefly in the police station in Nashville. I was there for urinating off a balcony or whatever songwriters did in those days, and she was there for *goniffing* seven packets of eyeliner or something from one of Nashville's finer department stores. She was well dressed, beautiful, and fragile in tears. Her makeup was running, so it was probably a pretty good thing that she'd lifted the eyeliner. Eventually, her slightly embarrassed corporate husband came down to get her just before she shoplifted my heart. But there was something about the way she looked at me as she left that now made me think of Winnie Katz. In those days it was sicker to be a lesbian than a kleptomaniac, but values are changing.

Obviously, attempting an affair with a lesbian is not particularly best foot forward. Of course, we did like some of the same things.

I lit another cigar and gently stroked the cat.

I must've done a few other things too, because before I knew it, Sunday night had rolled around, and I found myself listening to Ratso's rodentlike voice on the blower.

"Kinkster," he said, "I'm coming by to get you in the morning."

"Why?" I asked. "Where're we going?"

Ratso's voice had sounded vaguely ill at ease, and it was making me feel uncomfortable too.

There was a rather awkward pause. Then Ratso said, "It's a surprise."

I poured a healthy jolt from a nearby bottle of Jameson into the bull's horn. I don't like surprises worth a damn, but I liked the strange tone in Ratso's voice even less. It sounded like an uncharacteristic effort to be patronizing.

I killed the shot.

"Goody," I said.

11

▲▲▲

Monday morning I was warming up a rather elderly bagel when I heard what appeared to be screeching noises coming from the sidewalk below. I walked over to the kitchen window and looked down into the gray February drizzle. At first I didn't see anything. Then three dark forms began to emerge from the bleak background like blurry figures on a photographic plate.

I rubbed my eyes, opened the window, and looked again. Ratso, McGovern, and Rambam, a private investigator I'd sometimes worked with, were all standing on the sidewalk shouting up at me. They looked like three sullen leftover Christmas carolers.

"Throw down the fuckin' puppet head!" yelled Rambam.

I looked on top of the refrigerator, and there it was—the little black puppet head smiling stoically, with the key to the building lodged firmly in its mouth. A little homemade parachute was attached to the puppet head, and when I looked carefully, I noticed that so were a few cobwebs. That was all right. Puppets, like people, sometimes need to rest their weary heads.

I stood in front of the window and gazed fondly at the puppet head in my hand. To some, it was merely a puppet head. Others might think of it as an extremely short concierge. To me, it was a friend.

I threw my friend's head out the window at a slight angle, taking into consideration the way the freezing drizzle was pounding into the building from the south. It took a nice trajectory over the fire escape, drifted gently back toward Hudson Street, caught a little downdraft around the second-floor level, and Ratso came up with it like a desperate bridesmaid.

I got a brief glimpse of the dark expression on Ratso's face as he gripped the puppet head and looked back up at the window, and I realized the quiet weekend was o-v-e-r.

The psychiatrist's office was over on Charles Street, a short but, under the circumstances, extremely unpleasant taxi ride from the loft.

I did not need a shrink. What had occurred in Cleveland was enough to unhinge even a normal person, but every time I tried to bring it up in the cab, Ratso would say, "Tell it to Dr. Bock."

"But be sure not to tell him that we once burgled his office," said Rambam. His eyes were the color of steel, and they were looking at me as if I were a lab specimen. Apparently, I was being forcibly taken to the same shrink on whom we'd done a little B & E operation a few years back. That time, I needed the psychic goods on a croaked bisexual. This time, I didn't need a goddamn thing. Well, I'd tell that to Dr. Bock.

"It can't hurt to talk to him," McGovern said, as the four of us crowded into the little waiting room.

"Yes, it can," I said in a loud, hostile, petulant voice that brought the head of the grossly overweight receptionist slowly swiveling toward me like a large bird of prey. Ratso walked over to the desk and spoke to her, and I sat down and tried to make sense of what was rapidly becoming a rather tedious, not to say undignified, situation.

There were three of them, not counting the big receptionist and the little shrink, who was hiding in his hole somewhere, and there was only one of me, unless, of course, I had a multiple personality and there were several of me. I flatly doubted that. If I was that crazy, the cat would've left me long ago.

Suddenly, forged of necessity, I came up with a great idea. I'd humor my three so-called friends and tell Bock about John Morgan. Then I'd get Bock to hypnotize me. In my conscious mind the memories of Borneo and Morgan were about as faded as my old sarong, but in my subconscious there might just lay the key to the whole baffling situation. It couldn't hurt to try.

When the receptionist called my name, we all trooped into the shrink's office like the Von Trapp family climbing a hill, Ratso and McGovern both, apparently, wanting a prior word with the guy. Bock got up and came over to us, and we all went through the usual unpleasantries. Finally, Bock said curtly, "I wasn't aware this was a group-therapy session. I'll have to ask all of you, except Kinky, to please wait outside."

Ratso and McGovern nodded and left, as did Rambam, who, I noticed, had been futzing around in the vicinity of Bock's desk while all the team captains had been introducing themselves. He winked at me as he stepped into the waiting room.

A little over an hour later, I stepped into the waiting room myself, preshrunk, posthypnotized, and extremely pissed. I didn't remember a thing about the hypnosis, and Bock, citing professional ethics, had stubbornly refused to let me have the tape he'd made of the session.

"No tapes are to go out of the office at any time," he said dismissively. "Come back next week, and I can discuss it with you."

"Fat chance," I said rather thoughtlessly as I passed the receptionist. We all walked outside, except Ratso, who stayed behind, I later learned, to stick me with the bill. In troubled times, there are some constants.

"Jesus, I wanted to hear that tape," I said, shaking what was left of my head in disgust.

"Go back next week," said McGovern.

"No need," said Rambam, pointing to his attaché case. "I bugged the office."

I stopped and looked at Rambam with renewed admiration.

"Somewhere," I said, "H. R. Haldeman is smiling."

"... *I feel the nails going into my body* ... *I see the blood flowing out* ... *I see a multitude of people standing around me.* ..."

"Christ," Ratso said, as back in the loft we all listened to my voice on the tape, "maybe he's sicker than I thought." He looked across at me as I sat at my desk. I shrugged.

"Make it a little louder, will you?" McGovern shouted from the couch. Rambam walked over to the attaché case on the kitchen table and adjusted a knob on the little tape recorder.

"... *Oh, God, stop them* ... *they don't know what they're doing.* ..."

There was a silence on the tape. Ratso, Rambam, and McGovern were all staring at me. I moved uneasily in my chair. I tried to look relatively sane. This certainly wasn't what I'd expected to hear.

We all waited.

The next voice on the tape was Dr. Bock's. He sounded a bit surprised himself, possibly excited in a rather clinical way. Shrinks like a little variety too. He was asking me what I saw now.

"I can hardly wait," said Rambam.

"*. . . they are giving me more* tuak *to drink . . . more betel-nut to chew . . . Morgan is there . . . he is smiling as he hands me a stick of* ganja *. . . they are dipping the nails in pig fat . . . the people are crowding around me . . . I'm lying on the floor of the* ruai. *. . . I see two small Kayan boys who are identical, maybe eight years old . . . haircuts like little tadpoles . . . one is holding a bottle of* tuak *. . . the other is carrying banana leaves almost as big as he is . . . they are native boys, but they both have remarkable, frightening blue eyes . . . blue as the sky. . . . I want to ask a question, but I can't . . . the pain is coming back now . . . I am seeing explosions of light. . . . Morgan is here again. . . . Now they are wrapping my arm in banana leaves. . . . Morgan is talking to me. . . . 'Got some great shots,' he says. . . . I am looking at my arm, but all I see is blood and banana leaves. . . . I close my eyes . . . I hear Morgan saying, 'Great looking tattoo, man. Now your arm's got to be buried in a gentile cemetery.' . . .*"

"Maybe now," I said as I got up and poured drinks for the house, "you three doubting Thomases will finally come to believe that I do not think I'm Jesus Christ."

"Rather an inversion of the biblical theme," said McGovern, downing the shot, "but it does come as a relief."

"Yeah," I said, "and I want to say that your faith in me has been very heartening." I killed the shot and poured another one for McGovern and myself.

Ratso was still staring at his drink. "Well," he said, "at least we now know beyond a doubt that the John Morgan you claim to have known did exist. Let's see this tattoo of yours."

I pulled up my sleeve, and the three of them gathered around to look at the bluish markings on my left arm. "It's a Kayan stylized version of a dog," I said. "Here's the jaw, and these are the teeth. This is the eye of the dog," I continued, pointing to a marking at the center of the rather elaborate design. "When you die, it's supposed to become

a torch and light your way to heaven. It protects my soul."
McGovern knocked back his second shot. "It's got its
work cut out for it," he said.

We'd had a few more drinks, and McGovern and I were
carrying on a rather acrimonious debate about the Piers
Akerman scrotum incident, when suddenly I thought I
heard a woman's voice coming from the general area of the
attaché case.

"What was that?" asked McGovern.

"I told you," said Rambam. "I didn't just record Kinky's
session, I bugged the goddamn office. This is his next patient." Rambam smiled.

"Maybe we should turn it off," said McGovern.

"Let it run," said Ratso. "I've got a graduate degree in
deviant psychology. I'm interested."

"Too bad you didn't take a course in ethics," I said.

"C'mon," said Ratso, pouring himself another shot of
Jack Daniel's. I'd had to bring in reinforcements for the
bottle of Jameson we'd already killed. "This can't hurt
anybody. This'll be fun. Let it roll."

"So, Winnie," Dr. Bock was saying, "the last time we
talked, you were dealing with guilt feelings about your
fascination with a menage à trois involving Edith Piaf and
Mama Cass."

McGovern choked on his drink. Ratso and Rambam
laughed so hard we missed a little of the dialogue. I looked
up at the ceiling. At least it was quiet up there now.

The next thing we heard was a voice saying, "—no
longer bothers me. I've resolved that. I came to see you
today for another reason. But it's kind of embarrassing."

"Anything you say," said Dr. Bock firmly, "stays in this
room."

"I'll drink to that," said McGovern.

"Well, I've been breaking out in a rash all over my—all
over my body. It makes it quite uncomfortable to continue

giving my dance classes. When you wear tights and leotards and things and you're as physical as I am—well, you can imagine what it's like. Or can you?"

"Of course," said Dr. Bock.

"I've been to three doctors. I've tried everything. It goes away for a while, but it keeps coming back worse than ever."

"Sounds psychosomatic," said Dr. Bock. "Possibly related to childhood neglect, adolescent anxieties, adult guilt."

"But none of that bothers me, Dr. Bock. In fact, nothing seems to bother me except—"

"Except what, Winnie? Tell me."

"Except cigar smoke and cats," she said.

That night I wandered down to the Monkey's Paw alone, looked for trouble, didn't find any, and wandered back to 199B Vandam. They say if you're looking for trouble you'll find it, but the truth is, if you look too hard for anything you probably won't find it. The way you find stuff is not to look for it. You might even try praying for things you don't want. Run in a little reverse psychology on God. You could get lucky.

Of course, sometimes you want what you want.

On this particular evening I wanted some tuna for the cat and some fish ice cream for myself, but both of our cupboards were about as empty as Little Orphan Annie's irises. The cat peered under the counter with me, saw there was no cat food, and turned away in disgust. I offered her the bagel that I never got around to that morning, but she drew a bye. She had very little appreciation for ethnic things.

I had just taken off my boots and was thinking of making it an early night when the phones rang. No big deal. Happens to firemen all the time.

I walked across the cold wooden floor in my tie-dyed socks, which I'd bought from a guy at an arts fair who had a booth that sold nothing but tie-dyed socks. You can imagine what kind of drugs he'd taken in his life.

I made it to the desk and opted for the blower on the left. I almost always opt for the blower on the left. Partly because I'm left-handed, and partly because I'm a creature of narrow habit. Also, I've done pretty well in my life, all things considered, and I don't see any point in changing blowers in the middle of the stream.

It was Carmen. She was at the Pierre Hotel.

"Kinky," she said, "can you come over now? I'm scared."

"Soon's I get my boots on. What room are you in?"

"Eleven-oh-seven . . . I think there's someone following me. I saw him at the airport, and when I was checking in, I saw him in the hotel lobby."

"Could be coincidence. What's he look like?"

"He's an old man. . . . Maybe I'm wrong . . . but something about him gives me the goose bumps. He's wearing a dark suit with white socks and a blue flower in his lapel."

"Snappy dresser," I said.

I told her I'd be right over, and to stay in her room until I got there. I hung up, put on my boots, grabbed my hunting vest, coat, cowboy hat, and a few cigars for the road. I left the cat in charge, and headed out into the New York night.

It was after eleven when I hailed a hack on Hudson. A

light snow was starting to fall, and under the streetlights it looked almost timeless, like leftover Lindbergh confetti.

"Pierre Hotel," I told the driver, as offhandedly as I could.

There were shabbier destinations.

Whatever the Pierre may have lacked in soul, it made up for in opulence. It wasn't your down-home kind of place, but the people who stayed there weren't down and they weren't home, so why should they give a damn? The place welcomed a Claus von Bulow or a Zsa Zsa Gabor like the Statue of Liberty, but a guy coming in late at night with a cowboy hat, a hunting vest, and a cigar might have to search for the golden door farther downtown.

My friend Bill Osco from L.A. always stayed at the Pierre when he was in New York. Bill used to dress like most rich people in California: crummy jeans, crummy jacket, and a baseball cap. He told me once he'd stayed at the Pierre for two weeks, and every night when he'd come back to the hotel, a security guy in the lobby would come up to him and say, "Can I help you?" Bill would always answer, "Yeah. You can get out of my way so I can get to my room."

As I paid the cabbie and tipped the doorman, who was dressed like that archduke whose assassination started World War I, I visualized myself breezing through security, and damned if it didn't work. Two security guys were harassing some guy in a baseball cap, and I blew right by in a trail of cigar smoke. The lobby wasn't crowded. Nobody was wearing white socks and blue flowers. I found an open elevator, bootlegged the cigar inside, and pushed eleven.

A woman, probably in her late fifties, was already in the elevator. She was dressed like a dead teenager. It didn't take her long to flare her manicured nostrils, fix me with a haughty little moue of distaste, and march off the Otis box at four. You meet all kinds of people on elevators.

I got off at eleven, followed the gilded maze around for a while, and finally arrived at 1107. I started to knock, and realized that the door was not quite shut all the way. Rather careless of Carmen, I thought.

I knocked anyway. Nothing.

I walked in and saw that the room was part of a larger suite. Maybe Carmen was on the other side.

I walked through a kind of sitting room and went into the far end of the suite. A woman's belongings were strewn around, including a purse and a scarf on the floor. Rather sloppy of Carmen, I thought.

I picked up the purse and started to go through it. I felt vaguely like Art Linkletter rifling a strange woman's purse on his old TV show. There was something wrong with going through a woman's purse, even if you found it on the floor of a hotel room. But there are a hell of a lot of things in the world that are a hell of a lot wronger. I could see the reaction to one of them in my eyes in the wall mirror.

Her name was Carmen Cohen, I learned. Melodic name.

From a land where people disappear. Argentina, in this case.

Now Carmen Cohen had disappeared. I felt a sense of confusion mingling with the stronger sense of danger. I was in some kind of unfocused tableau, standing alone in a suite in the Pierre Hotel holding the purse of a strange woman who had disappeared before she could tell me anything about John Morgan, whom I couldn't seem to find either.

I didn't like puzzles that much. Especially those that appear increasingly to be cut from a large, raw, karmic chunk of evil.

"Maybe ten thousand young broads a week turn up missing in New York City," said Detective Sergeant Mort Cooperman as he poked rather desultorily through Carmen Cohen's suitcase. "Most of them, of course, aren't missing at all," he added as he gazed somewhat skeptically around the hotel suite.

"Most of them just stood up guys like you," said Detective Sergeant Buddy Fox from the doorway to the living room. The hotel dick standing next to him nodded his head like a mildly bored robot.

"Most of them," I said, "don't leave their purses behind when they go."

"See, I told you, Fox," said Cooperman with his back to us, "it ain't Kinky's purse." These guys had some sharp banter going.

Cooperman and Fox and I seemed to be fated foils. Circumstances had often thrown us together, and never had it been what you would call pleasant. Shucking all modesty, Ratso and I had arrived at solutions to a number of cases that had baffled the NYPD. To make matters worse, McGovern had flaunted our amateur crime-solving expertise in the *Daily News* to such an extent that Cooperman had probably thought twice before he'd saved my life in a rather terrifying caper the year before at Madison Square Garden. It became quite obvious at times that Cooperman wondered if he'd made the right decision.

This, it appeared, was to be one of those times.

Cooperman now turned to face the rest of us just as Ratso came running into the room, slightly out of breath, wearing lavender slacks, a sweater with little hockey players all over it, and a coonskin cap with the raccoon's face, eyes sewn shut, mounted on the front.

Cooperman shut his own eyes for a moment, possibly hoping the vision would go away. When it didn't, he spoke in a voice that sounded remarkably like the hiss of a subway train.

He said, "Terrific. Just terrific. The goddamn fucking Bobbsey Twins."

"What did I miss?" Ratso asked.

About five minutes later Cooperman motioned to Fox and they headed for the door. "We'll file a report," he said shortly.

"Wait a minute," I said. "We're dealing with a missing person here." I'd already told them about Carmen's call to me and about her fear that she was being followed by an old man with white socks and a blue flower. The story hadn't dented their demeanors noticeably.

"As far as we're concerned," said Cooperman, "she's not missing yet." Ratso and I stared in mild disbelief.

"And if she's any friend of yours," Fox said with a harsh little chuckle, "we're not sure she's a person yet."

"I'll sleep better knowing you guys're on the job," I said.

Cooperman turned in the doorway so he was facing me. His massive torso practically blotted out the hall. "If she doesn't turn up, call us back in twenty-four hours. Then she can be declared officially missing, and we'll open a file.

There's nothing else we can do now unless she's a minor, a senior citizen, or mentally incompetent." Cooperman turned and left.

"Like you," Fox added with a little leer. Then he followed Cooperman out to the elevators.

Ratso and I watched the hotel dick double-lock the room. Then we took an elevator down to the lobby.

"What do we do now?" Ratso asked.

"Make a phone call," I said.

"No problem," said Rambam, nodding confidently toward the C-note in his right hand. "I've got the master key to every room in the hotel right here."

The three of us were sitting in the downstairs bar of the Pierre knocking back whiskey at about six bucks a shot, and I wasn't counting on Ratso to pick up the tab. I'd told Rambam about the cops, the room, the phone call from Carmen, and, of course, the old man, the white socks, and the blue flower. The whole story seemed somehow to have a faint aura of unreality clinging to it.

"You guys sit tight," said Rambam, getting up from the table. "I'll just have a word with the bell captain."

"Make it a quick word," Ratso said. "They're closing this bar pretty soon, and loitering in that lobby's harder than it looks."

Rambam left, Ratso ordered another round, and I thought things over. With security the way it was, it would've been tough to get anyone out of the hotel against her will in the time frame in which we were working. I was betting that Carmen was still in the hotel. And if anybody knew the ins and outs of locked hotel rooms, it was Rambam.

I thought of the time, several years before, when Rambam had provided the final piece in the puzzle that would hang the infamous Hank Williams Killer at the Lone Star Cafe. To do that, he'd had to go unbeknownst into the murderer's locked hotel room. Of course, that had taken place at the Gramercy Park, and this was the formidable and mildly intimidating Pierre Hotel. This would be harder. Much harder. But sometimes in life, what one learns in St. Mary Mead does hold true in London. I had confidence in the boy.

Rambam returned just as the impeccably dressed waiter was shoehorning Ratso and me out of the bar. Over his shoulder he was carrying what looked like some dry cleaning with the hotel's fancy paper wrapper covering it. Under the dark gaze of the waiter he walked back into the bar, lifted his glass in a toast to the irritated man, killed the shot, and walked back out to where we were standing.

"One for the elevator," he said.

We walked over to an alcove near the elevators and sat in a plush forest of expensive-looking, uncomfortable furniture.

"Just like your loft," said Ratso.

"Just like room seventeen-oh-two," said Rambam.

"You think she's in there?" I asked.

"I don't know," said Rambam, "but that's the room of the old geezer with the white socks and blue flower. Bell captain thinks he's an old queen. Has the look, he says. Also, he saw him with two big blond hunks earlier this evening, so he may not be alone."

"Maybe they're all havin' an orgy up there," said Ratso.

"Maybe you can flash your *National Lampoon* press card

and they'll let you in," I said. Ratso tilted his coonskin cap to a rather rakish angle.

"Getting in is no problem," said Rambam. "The hard part, in this kind of situation, may be getting out."

"Room service," said the voice.

The man in the red-and-gold bellman's jacket balanced a tray of food with his right hand. With his left he knocked on room 1702.

"Room service," he said again, with just a very slight hint of an un-Pierrelike intonation. This time he knocked louder. Ratso and I were waiting about ten feet farther up the hall, but we clearly heard the irritated voice on the inside of the door.

"We didn't order any room service," it said, logically enough. I would've preferred that he'd said "I" instead of "we," but there wasn't much to be done about it now. Sometimes when you look for trouble you find it.

"Terribly sorry, sir," said Rambam with a dangerous-looking wink to me and Ratso. "If you'll please just sign the receipt and state that you didn't place the order. I have to account for the tray to the room-service captain."

The door opened a crack, and Ratso and I flattened ourselves against the wall. An unseen presence was checking Rambam out. I felt a small wave of pity for the guy behind the door. He had no way of knowing at that moment he was staring into the eyes of probably the most dangerous room-service waiter in America. Of course, at the time, I didn't know whom or what we were dealing with. Had I known that then, the little wave of pity would've been buried in a tidal bore of stronger, deeper emotion.

Then the door closed and I heard a muffled metallic noise that sounded like a chain being removed from a door, a weapon being cocked, or, barely possibly, the Tin Man getting a new heart.

The door opened.

A large blond head peered out like an Aryan turtle, radiating evil. The head had a vague familial resemblance to Gorgeous George, the wrestler. It swiveled in an almost mechanical fashion, and suddenly its furtive eyes, like smuggled emeralds, locked with my own. For a fraction of a second I saw a gleam that seemed to emanate from a great and chilling darkness. Then Rambam dropped the loaded tray on Gorgeous's head and rolled across the threshold like a vicious, conscienceless, somewhat larger model of the Little Engine that Could.

Ratso and I heard dull thuddings and muffled shouts as we headed for the open door. Gorgeous came squirting out of the room on two wheels, collided solidly with Ratso, and ricocheted off the wall. He fixed us with a shivery liquid gaze, and then ran down the hallway in the direction of the stairs.

"Forget him," I said, as Ratso slowly got back on his feet. "Let's find the girl."

The two of us were converging on the room again when Rambam yelled, "Watch out for Goldilocks!" A second man, blond and somewhat bloodied, came crashing through the doorway, hooking Ratso in the gut with his left shoulder. Ratso went down again. The guy bugged out for the dugout.

When Ratso and I finally got into the room, Rambam closed the door behind us. The right side of his face was beginning to resemble the color of his bellman's uniform, but otherwise he looked pretty cheerful. Ratso had taken off his coonskin cap and was trying to decide whether to hold his head or his stomach. The room was empty.

"If she's not in the dumper or the closet, maybe we did break up a poofter's convention," I said.

"One way to find out," said Rambam. "But I'm warning you, it could be ugly."

I pushed open the bathroom door and walked in. On the floor were a woman's shoes, stockings, skirt, and blouse. I walked back into the room just as Rambam was opening the closet.

"Door number three," he said as he pulled on the knob.

Inside the closet a woman was tied by the wrists to the clothes rod and gagged with a pillowcase. She was wearing nothing but a pair of lace panties. She was the most beautiful woman I'd seen since Jean Seberg had gone to Jesus.

Ratso dropped his coonskin cap and made no effort whatsoever to pick it up.

Whatever they'd doped Carmen with before they'd tied her up, I wouldn't have minded a few hits of myself. She was definitely out where the buses don't run. Ratso had done a fairly convincing job of getting her into a Pierre Hotel robe and laying her down on one of the beds. Now Rambam and I were studying the jacket that one of our blond friends had left behind in the room. We were studying it on Ratso's body, and he was studying it in the full-length mirror.

"It was probably Gorgeous's," I said. "He's about your size, and he left in a hurry."

"So did Goldilocks," said Rambam.

"Whatever did you say to him?" Ratso asked. He was going through the pockets of the coat and finding absolutely nothing.

After some time Ratso came up with a small scrap of paper. It was a receipt for a roll of film someone had dropped off at one of those quickie developing places.

"Couldn't have been Carmen," I said. "If she stayed in

the room like I told her, she wouldn't have had time."

"I'll ask her when she comes to," said Ratso.

"You do that," said Rambam. He was looking for labels in the jacket and finding none. "That's interesting," he said at last. "It's been sanitized."

"Yeah," said Ratso, looking at the fabric of the sleeve, "it's nice and clean, all right."

"That's not what I meant," said Rambam. " 'Sanitized' means somebody has taken the trouble to cut all the manufacturer's labels out of a garment. This guarantees anonymity, hides the country of origin and . . ." Rambam looked thoughtfully at the sleeping woman on the bed.

"And what?" Ratso asked.

"And means," said Rambam grimly, "that we could be in some deep, very unpleasant, international shit."

I took a few steps back and leveled a measured gaze at Ratso in the jacket.

"It's you," I said.

Tuesday morning broke dark and threatening over New York City. Actually, it was around eleven o'clock when I woke up. Morning, like anything else in this world, is relative. Some people had probably been up since 6:00 A.M. doing squat thrusts in the parking lot, eating fibered cereal, and disturbing other Americans with early morning phone calls. If you want to get up at 6:00 A.M. and pretend you're Tevye the Milkman, that's your problem. For me, morning begins when I realize that the soft warm body curled up next to me is a cat.

I looked out the bedroom window of the loft and couldn't decide whether it was the window that was grimy or the city. Then the events of the previous night came back to me, and I plunked down for the city. It's pretty hard to find good help willing to do cities these days.

As the espresso machine began to hum happily to itself, I lit a cigar and sat at the desk thinking thoughts as dark as the weather. Carmen was safely stashed away, for the moment at least, at Ratso's apartment in nearby Soho. Whoever was after her would know nothing of Ratso. It was a good place for her to stay for now, if she could stand living in a small apartment with a stuffed polar bear's head, a five-foot-tall statue of the Virgin Mary, three hundred hockey sticks, and roughly ten thousand books, the vast majority of them dealing with Bob Dylan, Jesus, or Hitler. The reason Ratso needed so many books was that none of them, quite understandably, attempted to deal with any more than one of the subjects. You rarely ever found a book about Jesus' influence on Hitler or about Bob Dylan's influence on Jesus. You couldn't very easily find an anthology that included more than one of them between its covers. In fact, there was only one thing I could think of that Jesus, Bob Dylan, and Hitler had in common, and that was that Ratso was an unrecognized world authority on all three.

Thunder rattled the warehouse doors of Vandam Street. I poured myself an espresso and proceeded to ponder particularly paranoid thoughts. Nothing really added up yet, but I was beginning to suspect that the phone call I'd received last week informing me of John Morgan's death might very possibly not have come from Cleveland. I didn't know why exactly I felt this, but the more I thought about it, the more likely it began to seem.

Maybe Carmen would provide us with the answers about John Morgan. It was 11:32 A.M. I called Ratso's number. The phone rang about five times, and I hung up before I had to listen to his gratingly familiar recorded voice.

Maybe they were both still dead to the world. Maybe they'd gotten up at six and were still doing squat thrusts in the parking lot. If I didn't hear from them in a while, I'd try again. At least Carmen was in safe, if slightly horny, hands.

I'd given the receipt for the roll of film to Rambam to pick up as soon as possible. If one of our blond friends wanted that film bad enough, I was sure he could pick it up without the receipt. I expected to hear from Rambam soon. I expected to hear from Ratso soon.

All I heard was the dull thudding of the lesbian dance class starting up over my head. It sounded vaguely like primitive drums answering the thunder. Man's answer to God. No, woman's answer to Mother Nature. Woman's answer to Father Nature? Whatever it was, it was tedious. But it was somebody's answer to something, which was a hell of a lot more than I had going for myself so far.

I got another cup of espresso and walked over to the kitchen window to watch the rain start to fall. At first it fell with a blue, glinty color, like the eyes of distant women. Then it came down harder and turned to a warm, and somehow comforting, New York gray. Tuesday's child smokes a cigar and watches the rain. There were worse ways to spend a Tuesday morning, I reflected, and in my life I'd tried more of them than I cared to remember.

The cat jumped up on the sill and watched the rain with me. I daydreamed that the cat and I were adrift on a ship in a dark and deep and dangerous ocean. What the cat daydreamed I do not know.

Dreams, they say, can never hurt you; only the dreamer can.

19

I was taking a little power nap on the couch—quite dreamless—when a voice from below, apparently gaining power as it spiraled upward through several concentric circles of urban hell, awakened me. I walked over to the window and looked down to see Rambam standing on the sidewalk. The rain had let up just a bit, but nonetheless he seemed to want the puppet head pretty badly. Pushy New Yorker if I ever saw one.

The puppet head and parachute were still a little damp from the day before, but I opened the window and floated it out with a flourish, like a Madison Avenue ad guy with a great new idea. It was a fairly nice shot, if I say so myself.

Running a puppet-head operation in the rain is not a casual proposition. It requires skills they don't teach you at vacation Bible college. It calls for a time-consuming and extremely high-maintenance relationship between man and puppet head. Of course, if it were easy, everyone would do it.

Rambam came in wearing a trench coat, like a spy in an old London Fog commercial. "I didn't know you guys really wore coats like that," I said.

"Oh yeah," he said. "It started many years ago in Europe and Latin America, when they had to wait around for a long time for puppets to fall." He flipped the slightly soggy puppet head over to me, and I replaced it carefully on top of the refrigerator.

Rambam tossed a packet onto my desk. "Photos," he

said. He walked over to the espresso machine and drew himself a cup. "Mulberry Street's got nothin' on you," he said.

"Keep the customer satisfied, I always say."

"I also got," he said, taking a healthy slurp, "some information on who rented the room last night at the Pierre. Between the bell captain, the room clerk, and several other less savory sources, this case is starting to get a little expensive."

"Put it on my tab," I said.

"That's what I was afraid you'd say," said Rambam. He studied his espresso leaves. Then he said, "The room was rented to the 88 Leasing Corp. out of Bayonne, New Jersey. That mean anything to you?"

"Place to start," I said. I walked over to the desk, took a cigar out of Sherlock's head, lopped the end off it with my cigar guillotine, and set fire to it with a kitchen match, always careful to keep the tip of the cigar well above the flame. Then I opened the packet of photos. Rambam wandered in behind me and glanced down at them over my shoulder.

The first shot was of a tree with what looked like some kind of chalk-marked symbol on it. Maybe an upside-down version of the peace sign the hippies used to use back when peace was happening. I'd almost forgotten what it looked like. Most of the pictures were jungle shots—banana trees, rubber trees, trees big enough for Tarzan's condo, overgrown trails, muddy rivers. There were several shots of what appeared to be an Indian cave painting. The painting looked vaguely Mayan at a glance—sunbursts, primitive animals, the Indian peace sign that was later inverted to make the swastika, a group of stick figures that might've been the ancient ancestors of Sherlock Holmes's dancing men.

In the middle of the roll somewhere there was one

terrific shot of John Morgan that nearly brought a tear to my eye. He was smiling from the front seat of a Land Rover pulled off to the left side of a small highway with the jungle rising all around it. On the right side of the road, going in the opposite direction, was a bus with about ninety-seven passengers, not counting chickens and goats. The bus looked like it had once belonged to Ken Kesey. I stared again at John's face. His hair was falling over his eyes, like always, but you could still see that they were sparkling, also like always, with mischief. Sun was dappling his features. He looked happy. That was how I remembered him.

I glanced at the remaining photographs. There was one of two old men standing around wearing panama hats. One of them had a rather prominent gap between his two front teeth. There were no more shots of John. The last picture was the same as the first, a similar chalk marking on the side of a tree. That was the lot.

"Standard South American jungle shots," I said. "Twenty-four pictures to the roll. No way to accurately date when they were taken."

Something was bothering me about the photographs. Like a troublesome insect that somehow had slipped under your mosquito net and wouldn't go away. I'd go over the pictures more thoroughly, I thought, after I'd had a chance to talk with Carmen, but something seemed wrong to me. I just didn't know what the hell it was.

At last I put the photos back in the packet. "You've seen one jungle," I sighed, "you've seen 'em all." I leaned back in my chair and puffed thoughtfully on the cigar.

"What's even stranger than these photographs," said Rambam, "was what the guy at the photo place said to me after I picked them up."

"What'd the guy say?"

"He said, 'Thank you, Mr. Morgan.'"

20

"Hello," I said. "This is Dr. Hiram Dickstein. I'm a corporate psychologist."

The woman's voice on the other end of the blower did not sound overly impressed.

"Yes," she said.

"This *is* the Secretary of State's Office?"

"Yes."

"In Trenton, New Jersey?"

"Yes." Large vocabulary.

"I need some information," I said, "on a new corporation. The 88 Leasing Corp."

"I can give you what we have on file. Just a moment, please."

I waited. It was almost four o'clock and I still hadn't heard from Ratso. Thoughtful of him to keep in touch. I picked up a half-smoked cigar out of my Texas-shaped ashtray and fired it up. Quite often they were better that way. Quite often a lot of things were better that way. The lady came back on the line.

"Yes, Dr. . . . uh . . ."

"Dickstein."

"Yes, well, I can give you the service address at the time of incorporation." She read out a lawyer's name and a street address in Bayonne, New Jersey, which I jotted down in my Big Chief tablet. "It's an active corporation, but it's not a new one. In fact, it's quite old."

"How old?"

"According to the card file, it was incorporated in 1946."

I thanked her and hung up. Interesting, I thought. For a company started in 1946, the 88 Leasing Corp. was a strange name.

So, of course, was Dr. Hiram Dickstein.

Around five o'clock I went out for a while to get some cat food and some Kinky food. I bought the cat food at a little corner grocery store on Tenth Street near Sheridan Square that was run by friendly foreigners who specialized in cat food and beer. I had dinner—party of one—at a little coffee shop on the square. They gave me a nice table by the window.

The rain-wept sidewalks of the Village shined like mirrors with lines. You could almost see yourself. I wondered if I'd always be a party of one. I wondered if I'd be an old man with a bow tie sitting alone on New Year's Eve looking out the window of some little restaurant at two dogs hosing on the sidewalk. That was certainly something to look forward to.

I walked across the square—past two panhandlers, an albino Negro, and an identically dressed matched pair of homosexuals, all loitering in the park. I thought about loitering myself for a while, but I was afraid I might fit in, so I walked over to the Monkey's Paw. It was a good place to drink and, on a slow night, it was a good place to think. It was a slow night.

Where was John Morgan? I wondered. In South America? In Borneo? In a Cleveland bone orchard? Lurking somewhere in New York? The boy reportedly got around pretty good, but this was ridiculous. Maybe the question should be: Who is John Morgan?

I sipped a Bass ale and turned an empty shot glass of Jameson thoughtfully in a clockwise direction on the mahogany. Carmen Cohen was the key to the puzzle. By now, with any luck, Ratso might have gotten all the answers out of her. The only other active lead, besides the photographs, was the service address of the 88 Leasing Corp. in Bayonne, New Jersey. That was the lawyer's office. So my two best leads were a lawyer and a woman, both, of course, inherently capable of treachery and deceit. Well, you work with what you've got.

When I arrived back at the loft, it was pretty late. I'd done more thinking than I thought. There was a message from Ratso on the machine. His experience with Carmen had been "very revealing" so far. He wanted to "explore further" some things with her. At the moment, according to the message, Ratso and Carmen were attending a party at the Egyptian embassy. He could get me in, too, he said, if I desired.

I desired to go to bed. The Egyptians had managed without me for thousands of years, and it was my guess they'd make it one more night. Egyptian culture had been pretty much downhill anyway ever since the Hebrews left for the suburbs.

I was in bed dreaming of pharoahs and kings when the phone rang like a sacred cat shrieking inside a tomb. It was Dylan calling me from Texas.

He'd remembered something.

"The four of us," Dylan was saying, "had left from Sibu on a trip to try to find the legendary headwaters of the Ulu Ayer. There were six of us in the longboat: Shanahan, Jones, Morgan, myself, and two Iban guides. We had a three-pronged giant hook with us that Shanahan intended to impale a chicken on and troll for crocodiles along the way. We had an RAF silk parachute that made into a great tent in the *ulu* if we needed it. We had supplies for two weeks. The only thing I'd forgotten was my little yellow pills for malaria.

"About six days into the journey we stopped at one of the last civilized outposts on the river, an Iban longhouse. We quickly became friends with the *tuai rumah,* the chief. They were having a festival for the eclipse of the moon, and *tuak* was offered to all of us. As you know, to refuse anything offered to you in the *ulu* is seen as an insult. Not drinking *tuak* is the sign of a woosie. Drinking until you vomit and then coming back and drinking some more is the sign of a real man."

"I wonder what they think of quiche," I said. I was propped up on the pillows and beginning to get into Dylan's story. I remembered that Dylan's *ulu* stories were always pretty good, but seldom if ever short-winded.

"So we're all sitting on the *ruai,* everybody—even the little children—are drinking and smoking bark-wrapped jungle tobacco, and the moon is slowly being gobbled up by a *hantu*—a local ghost of some kind—and all around us people are beating gongs. A few of them are playing the *sapei*—you know, the three-stringed native guitar—and dancing the *najhat.*

"So, suddenly, Jones, who's sitting right in the middle of the whole group, throws his legs over his head and shouts to nobody in particular, 'Light me.' Nobody makes a move. Jones shouts at the top of his lungs, 'Light me!' Shanahan reaches over with a cigarette lighter to Jones's ass and lights it. Jones promptly blasts about a six-inch-long blue darter. One of the best I've ever seen. The Ibans, of course, were completely blown away by it, in more ways than one. It was a form of magic from the red-haired devil that they'd never seen before. It was a little like when the American Indians first saw a demonstration of gunpowder.

A very sharing and caring experience culturally speaking."

"Fine," I said. I knew better than to tell Dylan to get to the meat of it. He was so into his story that he'd forgotten to speak in song lyrics.

"Anyway, later that night Shanahan decides he's going to try to *niap* one of the native girls. We've all been drinking pretty heavily. A lot of people have already passed out. So a mischievous Iban friend of Shanahan's points to a certain door of a *rumah*, Shanahan tries it and it's locked. So the Iban tells him how to climb over the inside wall of the longhouse and jump down into the *rumah* where the young *prempaun* is sleeping.

"About five minutes later we hear a loud cracking noise—you know, the floors are made of bamboo slats—and we all rush over to the door, the *prempaun* opens it, and there's a big hole in the floor. We look into the hole and there's nothing. Silence and blackness. Those longhouses, you know, are built on stilts, some of them are twenty to thirty feet off the ground, or more. So we all go racing down the *ruai*, down the log plank—which is actually easier to do when you're *mabbok* than when you're sober—and we start looking desperately for Shanahan under the longhouse. We're sure he's broken his neck. Finally, we find him facedown in about two feet of pig shit. We get him up and he's all right. All he says is, 'Terrific hose.'

"About an hour later only the *tuai rumah* and I are still drinking. Everybody else is passed out. The chief is really taking a shine to me because I'm staying with him on the *tuak*. So when we finally crash, he brings me into his own *rumah* and lets me sleep in his own bed. He goes somewhere else. The bed is a beautiful four-poster job like you might find in an elegant old hotel in the States. I don't know where he got it. Anyway, in the middle of the night I start feeling really sick. I get up and I stagger as far as I can and I vomit. Then I find my way back to the bed and I'm out for the night.

"In the morning, when I went out on the *ruai*, everybody in the longhouse was laughing. 'What is it?' I asked. 'You vomited on the chief,' they said."

I told Dylan to hang fire, got up and found a cigar and the ashtray in the shape of the state of Texas, and scampered back into bed. I usually didn't like to smoke in bed, but this was a special occasion. Not that Dylan's story wasn't humorous. It was just that it was longer than the Punic Wars. I lit the cigar.

"Start talkin'," I said.

"It was true. He'd given me his bed, and he'd slept on the floor near the bed. But he was a good sport—he didn't try to take my head or anything. Of course, they had about thirty or forty heads already, hanging in woven baskets from the rafters of the *ruai.* "

"It all sounds like good public-relations work," I said. "What happened next?"

"Okay," said Dylan. "We go upriver the next day, and we start hearing stories about this great white tiger with blue eyes. It's a *hantu*, you know. There are no tigers in Borneo. There are panthers, orangutans, cobras—"

"An old British ex-pat once told me," I said, "that the most dangerous animal in the jungle is the bee."

"The bee?"

"The bee. A swarm of bees in the *ulu*, if it comes after you, means almost certain death, my lad."

"Well, *be* that as it may," said Dylan, "as we continued upriver, we kept hearing stories from the natives about the great white tiger with the blue eyes. I was starting to have dizzy spells, which, at the time, I mistakenly attributed to *tuak* consumption rather than malaria. I began suggesting that, as long as we were so close to the headwaters, we take a hard left when we got there, and go in search of the white tiger. This would take us, of course, through primary jungle, into an area quite unfamiliar to the Iban guides, just out of reach of Kayan country, and inhabited, supposedly, solely by nomadic Punans, who, as you know, are the only true pygmies of Borneo.

"They all said I was crazy."

"Pretty judgmental of them, wasn't it?" I said. "Pray continue."

"Well, two mornings later, I showed them. Just before dawn one of the guides and I packed up our *barang* and took our share of the supplies—enough, we thought, to get across the Kayan country—and set out through thick primary *ulu* searching for the lair of the white tiger. We left a note in the longboat for the others. I don't know if it was stubbornness or malaria that goaded me to make the trip, but all I can tell you is that I'm very lucky to be alive.

"The *ulu* was so thick that you could go for hours without even seeing the sun. It was like nothing I'd ever seen. By evening of the first day, I was getting cold chills and dizzy spells, and I knew I was running a fever. The whole first day we'd seen no sign of man except for a sacred-hornbill sculpture in a small clearing.

"Toward the evening of the second day we saw something very strange. A fog seemed to be rolling in through the jungle—cold, dense, and—it was the damnedest thing—it seemed to have a kind of life to it. It set the Iban's eyes to rolling, and it gave me a rather severe case of the goose bumps, I can tell you. Of course, it could've been the malaria. Even today, I'm not quite sure.

"Anyway, suddenly, in the middle of a nearby clearing, the fog parts and I see the biggest tiger I have ever seen—in or out of a zoo. It is white as driven snow, and its eyes, about the size of durians, are like pools of blue amber. Trapped in the amber, I can see something horrible beyond imagination screaming to get out. . . ."

"Of course," I said, clearing my throat, "it could've been the malaria."

"Don't bet on it, hoss. But I'll grant you, it is possible. Anyway, that's not the end of the story. When I came to, the sun was shining brightly. I was on my back in some kind of clearing. I sat up and looked around for the Iban guide, but he was gone like a gray goose in winter. Couldn't blame him.

"Suddenly, I was surrounded by the strangest-looking men I'd ever seen. Not Punans. Too tall. Not Ibans. Not Kayans."

"Kenyahs, maybe," I said.

"Maybe. But whatever the hell they were, I could have sworn that several of them—if I hadn't known better—had looked at me and then given me a Nazi salute."

"Could've been the malaria," I said, but a chill tumbled its way like a miniature Austrian avalanche down the slopes of my spine. Neither of us spoke for a moment.

"You still with me, hoss?" Dylan asked.

"I'm afraid so," I said.

"Well, I got out of there alive, I'm not sure I even remember how exactly, and six months later I'm telling the story to a group of people in a bar in Kuching. Shanahan, Jones, and Morgan are there, and a few others—Dick Myers, John Schwartz, Jim Murchison, Chris Cooke. By the time I get to the end of the story, everybody's blown away. Everybody except Morgan, who sits there quietly nodding his head. 'Could be some kind of anthropological land bridge,' he says."

"Sure," I said. "An anthropological land bridge. Kind of like throwing away your beads and singing 'Oh, Susanna.'"

"Yeah," said Dylan. "I didn't think much of the idea either. But get this. Two months later I'm leaving the country for good, going back to the States. I'm trying to check up on a few friends before I leave. I couldn't find anybody who'd seen Morgan. So I call your old friend Effendi bin Addis—you were on leave in Thailand at the time, remember, so I didn't see you when I left. I ask Effendi where Morgan is, and guess what he says?"

"Morgan's lighting farts in a mosque in Brunei?"

"Not quite, hoss. Effendi says he's afraid our boy's gone completely *gilah*. He says Morgan's up at the headwaters of the Ulu Ayer. Effendi says Morgan's gone hunting for a white tiger with blue eyes."

Wednesday morning I got up on the wrong side of the bed. That was how I found my IMUS IN THE MORNING coffee mug. I stepped on the bastard, slipped, and damn near broke my neck. Household accident #467. Obviously, a broad had left it there on some recent memorable evening that had slipped my mind. I wound up on the floor, and the mug wound up under the bed.

As I looked for it, I also found myself surreptitiously checking for Nazis, communists, Jehovah's Witnesses, and a few other things that I didn't need lurking on the dark side of my life. Of course, ever since I was thirty-seven years old, I haven't been the kind of person who looks under his bed. I believe so much weird stuff that can mess up your life happens *in* the bed that anything happening underneath is going to need all the help it can get.

I found the mug, kicked the espresso machine into low gear, and frisbeed the fairly fossilized bagel out the window onto Vandam Street, narrowly missing a small group of tourists. I don't know what they were doing on Vandam Street. Maybe they were lost. Unless they came from a country that greatly admired garbage trucks, there was no reason for them to be there.

The reason I knew they were tourists is because they

were dressed a little better than your average New Yorkers and they were walking slow and looking at things. Nobody from New York walks slow and looks at things.

Of course, if the bagel had carried a little more to the left, I could imagine the front page story in the *Athol, South Dakota, Gazette:* LOCAL MAN KILLED BY FLYING BAGEL. Well, that was another thing to watch out for in the big city.

When the espresso was ready, I poured a cup, lit up a cigar, and sat down at the kitchen table to read yesterday's fish wrappers. It didn't take long for my attention to wander.

I didn't think there were Nazis under my bed, and I didn't really believe there were Nazis currently weaving their dark and bloody threads into the Made in the U.S.A. fabric of my life. Maybe their shadows were still hiding somewhere in the inside pockets of my youth, but as for them being my modern-day adversaries, I just didn't see it. There's a little bit of Nazi, I thought, and a little bit of Jew in all of us. How we deal with these diverse parts of our being will have a lot to do with what kind of lives we will eventually lead and what kind of world we'll be able to make for our children and our kittens.

I walked over to the desk and called Ratso. It was a deeply gratifying experience to finally be able to speak to him in person. We made plans to meet at La Bonbonniere, or La Lobotomy, as we sometimes called it, on Eighth Avenue at 11:00 A.M. It was agreed that he would come to breakfast alone. I knew almost nothing about Carmen Cohen, and it wasn't unthinkable that she was not who she represented herself to be. Few people are, when you think about it.

As I fed the cat and got ready to leave, it was dawning on me that, possibly for the first time, I might actually be needing Ratso's help. Of course, he'd helped me before, but that had usually been in a rather Watsonlike manner, showing me quite clearly how not to think, what not to do. As far as Carmen went, I would see what Ratso had learned, and then make arrangements to talk to her myself.

But it was in a deeper way that I now found myself needing Ratso's rather eclectic help. And a grim understanding was coming to me that this help would not be in regard to Bob Dylan or Jesus.

Sometimes, when darkness is moving in all around you, you don't see it because you've been looking for something else. In reality, the darkness has been there all the time, but you don't notice it until it is too late for daylight savings time to reach the western states of your soul.

The light goes down to low interrogation. Then it disappears almost completely, leaving only a candle, shaped maybe like a mushroom, made by the last hippie in the world. Then, quickly, the darkness rises up, snuffing out the candle, suffocating the spirit, and drowning you, inexorably, in an India inkwell of ancient evil.

That's what happens, sometimes, when you look under the bed.

"Nice jacket," I said to Ratso as we sat at one of the little tables near the window. At La Lobotomy, all the tables were near the window. Ratso's jacket was the color of phlegm.

"Thirty-seven dollars on Canal Street," he said, not without some pride. "Let's order."

Charles, the cook and proprietor of the place, took our orders for breakfast. Charles was one of the few Frenchmen I liked, and that was because he was probably a Greek.

Charles is a French name and La Bonbonniere is a French name, but the cuisine and ambience of the place were more like a Greek coffee shop than a French restaurant. I like Greek coffee shops more than French restaurants. They're more American.

Charles brought us our coffee. "I don't think," said Ratso, "that Carmen knows much more than we do about all this."

"That's great," I said. "Of course, she knows something. She knew to come here looking for me, didn't she? Maybe you're just a weak Watson."

"Maybe," said Ratso. "Maybe you're just an unpleasant Sherlock." He sipped his coffee.

"Look, Ratso, you've had plenty of time to get close to her."

"I *have* gotten close to her."

"That's what I was afraid of. I expected better of you Watson."

We drank our coffee in silence until Charles brought our breakfast.

I chewed a piece of very crisp bacon rather thoughtfully and watched as Ratso cut his eggs into ridiculously small segments with a knife and fork. It was not a particularly pleasant thing to see. I waited.

Ratso put a very large piece of ham into his mouth and gestured with his hand that the Heimlich maneuver would not be necessary. I waited.

Ratso took his time. He chewed, swallowed, belched, and said, "Morgan told her that at times his job could be dangerous. Not only dangerous to himself, he said, but quite possibly even dangerous for her. He didn't say what the job *was* and apparently she didn't push him on it."

"Unlikely."

"Anyway, if something went terribly wrong, he was to leave her a prearranged signal, and she was to leave Argentina as soon as possible. She was not to contact the embassy, the Peace Corps, or anyone else. She was to locate John's old friend from Borneo, a guy named Kinky, who could usually be found in Texas or New York. He'd know what to do."

I didn't know what to do. I stared mutely at Ratso and ate another piece of very crisp bacon.

"The prearranged signal," said Ratso, "was some sort of symbol to be written on a certain tree in Carmen's front yard."

On an impulse I took the package of photographs out of the pocket of my hunting vest and dealt the top photo across the table to Ratso. The one with the chalk marks on the tree in the jungle.

"Something like this?" I asked.

Ratso looked at the photo, then looked at me. "Yeah," he said thoughtfully. "I'll show this to Carmen."

"Not yet," I said, taking back the photograph. "These are deep waters, my dear Ratso. There's something I have to do first, and then I'll be wanting to speak to Miss Cohen myself. How's she holding up, by the way?"

"As well as could be expected. She's really a fine person, Kinkster." Ratso's face lit up like a harvest moon over Reno.

"No doubt. Now, Ratso, there's something I need your help with. I know you've been eager to tackle a case that deals with Bob Dylan, Jesus, or Hitler, and I just might have something that falls rather neatly into one of your arcane pockets of knowledge."

"Great! Which one?"

I took a sip of coffee and looked at Ratso for a moment. "I could be off on the wrong track, but if I'm correct, you can forget about Mr. Tambourine Man and the Baby Jesus."

Ratso stared at me like I was trying to take away his breakfast. "Jesus," he said.

"Forget about Him, I told you." Charles came over,

refilled our coffee, and went back behind the counter. "Something about that 88 Leasing Corp. rings a distant bell. It may be nothing, but check out that name 88 in relation to your third area of expertise."

"Okay." Ratso looked unconvinced but willing. His attitude, in truth, wasn't far off the mark from my own. When it came to wild notions of conspiracy and intrigue, I was usually from Missouri myself. Unless the conspiracy or intrigue took place in Missouri. Then I didn't believe it at all.

"Finally, Ratso, as we conclude the minutes of this Kiwanis breakfast, what else did you find out from Carmen about John Morgan?"

"Nothing. He was her fiancé. They had this prearranged signal—"

"Ratso, I went to Cleveland last week to bury an old and dear friend of mine. I can't tell you what it was like to look down into his coffin and see the body of a total stranger. Then, out of the blue, I hear from this broad in Argentina, who is the one human link that I have to what became of John Morgan. She comes to New York. She's immediately kidnapped, and God knows what else would've happened to her if we hadn't come along just when we did. Then I entrust her to my friend Ratso, who takes her to a party at the Egyptian embassy. Why not take her to lunch at the Carnegie Delicatessen with Henny Youngman?"

"That's this afternoon," said Ratso.

"Well, goddamnit, I wanted you to pump her." I must have raised my voice a little more than I thought, because an elderly lady at a nearby table wagged her finger at me. I could live with it.

Ratso was laughing. "I thought you said *hump* her," he said.

I smiled and got out a cigar. But I could see that I was going to have to talk to Carmen myself very soon. Any information we'd get from her was not likely to come through Ratso. Something in his eyes told me it was too late to tell him not to get too attached.

As Charles brought the check, an interesting thing occurred. It was sort of like a prearranged signal. Ratso went for the door at almost precisely the same moment that I went for my wallet.

Frank Sinatra never sang about Bayonne, New Jersey. The only music I heard as Rambam's black Jag rolled through the gray early dawn streets was a symphony of quiet desperation. It was 5:00 A.M., and the graveyard shift was on at the Dunkin' Donuts. In the near distance factories labored inexorably through the night to reverse photosynthesis. It looked like the kind of place Richard Corey might've grown up in.

"Not a garden spot, is it?" I asked, as we passed two cops sleeping in a patrol car on a side street.

"No," said Rambam, "and it doesn't smell like a garden, either."

"Wouldn't know. I haven't smelled anything in seven years."

"Roll down your window and you'll be born again."

We drove in silence for a while along a grimy corridor of unhappy-looking warehouses that obscured a city of dreaming Americans. If you had to dream, Bayonne was as good a place as any.

Earlier in the day I'd given Rambam the name of the lawyer and the service address for the 88 Leasing Corp. as faithfully transcribed in my Big Chief tablet. That afternoon Rambam had checked out the building and the attorney who represented 88. The building, he said, was a two-story converted warehouse that, in Rambam's words, would represent "no problem." The matter of the lawyer was even more interesting. He'd been dead for twenty years, but he was still paying the rent.

Rambam wheeled the Jag into a small alley down the street from a two-story office building that had been a warehouse when the world was young. No lights were on in the building as far as I could tell.

"I'm going to the pay phone on the corner to make a call to the law firm and the plumbing-supply company on the first floor. Make sure nobody's home. If a cop comes by, duck. If anybody else comes by and seems suspicious to you, honk."

"What if a panzer tank comes by and seems suspicious to me?"

"Call General Patton on the car phone," Rambam said, and disappeared into the gloom. I waited. I noticed there wasn't a car phone.

In a few moments Rambam was back. He opened the trunk, took out a green military knapsack and a long, ugly-looking pair of wire cutters, and vanished again. Scarcely three minutes later he reappeared and motioned for me to come with him. I got out of the Jag and crept along behind him toward the back of the building. The Hardy Boys in New Jersey.

Phone wires to the building were dragging on the ground. The door stood open about six inches. "That's the alarm system," said Rambam, gesturing to the wires, "and this is the door."

"What took you so long?" I asked as I followed him down a short hallway.

Rambam turned on a small flashlight. We climbed the stairs to the second floor and came to another hallway that appeared to have three or four offices opening into it. The 88 Leasing Corp. was not listed on any of the doors, but one door had a familiar name on it. The lawyer had been dead for twenty years, but his name was still on the door. It wasn't immortality, but it wasn't bad.

Rambam took a tool from his knapsack, which looked like it had been made for gutting catfish in a previous life. He did not get to use it, however. As he put his hand up to test the door, it swung open before our eyes like a vampire's vault.

"Strange," muttered Rambam. But strange, as we would soon find, was relative.

Rambam shone the small penlight around the dead lawyer's office. There was an old desk, a number of metal filing cabinets, and a lot of dust. The light cut the gloom just enough to reveal an open doorway into an adjoining room. We walked over to the doorway, and Rambam poked the light inside the room.

There was an object in the middle of the floor. I blinked my eyes a couple times, but it didn't go away.

"Jesus Christ," I said in a voice I almost didn't recognize.

The object on the floor was a man with two heads. Both of them looked very dead.

I felt a ghost train shuddering silently along my nerve tracks.

"Two heads are better than one," said Rambam.

As a kid in the dusty summertime, I vividly remember my visits to the Frontier Times Museum in Bandera, Texas. Years later, Piers Akerman, as a large adult Australian, visited the museum and called it "the attic of the town." That it certainly was, and more.

I remember kind old Mr. Hunter showing us the shrunken head of a South American Indian. It was about the size of a matzo ball, and the hair on the thing had continued to grow at approximately the rate of an inch a year. By now it must have some pretty amazing moss.

Mr. Hunter also had a wonderful collection of bells from around the world. He used to ring each one for us. Tibetan temple chimes, Chinese gongs, sleigh bells, cowbells, etc. That was many years ago, and Mr. Hunter has long since gone to Jesus, but sometimes, in a reflective moment in New York City, I can still hear the bells ring.

But the exhibit in the museum that truly hypnotized me and caused me to stare for long minutes at a time in transfixed horror was a freak two-headed goat in a glass case. Somehow the eyes of the animal—all four of them—looked almost evil in their innocence. For some inexplicable reason that little goat symbolized to me what could happen to man or beast if, as Sherlock Holmes says, "he leaves the straight road of destiny."

Now, decades later, in another time and almost another world, I stared with the same mixture of wonder and horror at the ghastly sight on the floor of the dingy office building in Bayonne, New Jersey. The four dead eyes leered back into the little tunnel of light pouring from Rambam's flashlight. I'd seen dead eyes before, and they're about as pleasant as watching Ratso eat eggs. But these were in a class by themselves. They seemed to struggle out of their sockets in a stalklike, insectine terror.

Rambam and I stepped a little closer. From this angle the creature looked like a radioactive crab on LSD. Both its faces were a healthy purple—healthy if you were an eggplant. Both faces were grinning, quite literally, from ear to ear. *Sardonicus* smiles. Probably nothing to a big-city coroner, but to your average American it was the kind of thing that, as Dorothy Sayers once observed, "could set one off one's nice beef steak."

As we walked a bit nearer to the creature, something about it, oddly enough, seemed to strike me as familiar. I knew the faces. I'd seen them before. As my eyes adjusted to the gloomy little room, it became readily apparent, much to my relief, that we were not dealing with a man with two heads. We were dealing with two men—our blond friends from the Pierre Hotel—who'd been tightly bound back to back and dispatched from this earth in a fashion most hideous. One blond head had lolled over at an impossible angle to create the eerie illusion of a two-headed man.

But both of them were certainly dead. And death, however you looked at it, was no illusion.

"Poison?" Rambam asked.

"Maybe it was salmonella," I said.

We looked at the bodies up close. I decided beyond any possible doubt that I was never going to be a big-city coroner when I grew up.

"What now?" I asked, as I followed Rambam back into the main office.

"We do a Jim Rockford. We get out of here. I'll dial nine-one-one on the phone and just put it down on the desk. The cops'll trace it and maybe they'll show up. I'm not going to get my voice recorded."

"I know what you mean," I said. "I'm between labels myself."

Rambam made the call, put the phone down on the desk, and headed for the door. I was on my way out with him when I noticed something lying in the dust beside an old hat rack that would've been at home in Elliot Ness's office. It was a feather.

I picked it up and was startled to see its very distinctive alternating brown and white bands of color.

"Hold the weddin'," I said, turning the feather incredulously in the palm of my hand. Rambam came back and took a look.

"Probably fell out of somebody's skypiece," I said.

"Or Big Bird from Sesame Street was here. Let's go."

"Okay," I said, "but there's only one kind of feather in the world that looks like this. And there's only one place you can find it. It comes from the sacred hornbill—the bird that's worshiped by the natives of Borneo."

"We don't get out of here now," said Rambam, "you'll see how that story plays down at the cop shop."

We left New Jersey on the wings of dawn. The hornbill feather was safely tucked away in the pocket of my hunting vest. But all the way home I thought I could hear the faintest of flutterings in the back of my consciousness. I recognized them for what they were. The wings of the Angel of Death.

It felt very reassuring to wake up late Thursday morning and know I was back in the good old wholesome Big Apple. It didn't feel good enough to click my heels together and say, "There's no place like home," but it was all right. The only people who might've been inclined to click their heels together were Dorothy in *The Wizard of Oz* or a Nazi. Maybe Dorothy was a Nazi. I resisted the urge to see if she was under my bed. Instead, I made some espresso and called McGovern.

"National desk," said the familiar voice from the blower on the left.

"I don't know if you remember me," I said. "Name is Kinky. Curly-headed fellow from Texas . . . played the guitar . . ."

"Of course," said McGovern. "You used to sleep on my

couch." He laughed louder than people normally laugh in the morning.

"Nothing slips by you, does it, McGovern?"

"Nothin' but the scenery on the A-train, baby. What do you need?"

"Two guys got themselves croaked in Bayonne last night. Maybe you could talk to one of your colleagues on the *Bayonne Bugle* or whatever it's called and get me a little inside information. I know there's a kinship between members of the Fifth Estate, and—"

"It's the *Fourth* Estate," said McGovern a bit testily. "Think of it this way. There's the First Amendment, the Second Coming, the Third Reich, and the Fourth Estate."

"That's a handy mnemonic. Look, McGovern, just give me some of the stuff they always hold back from the story. And check with the Coroner's Office too, will you?"

"I'm sort of your leg man, right?"

"Of course not, McGovern. You're not just a leg man. You play a vital role in determining what kind of poison would make two stiffs smile like Dr. Sardonicus."

"Jesus Christ. You saw them yourself?"

" 'Fraid so. And they weren't just saying 'Have a nice day.' "

"Well, I'm only your leg man. It's not really my business what you were doing in Bayonne in the middle of the night or whether it involves that friend from Cleveland you've been looking for who might or might not be dead. But you better pace yourself, pal. That's three stiffs in under a week."

McGovern said he'd call as soon as he had something. I hung up, sipped a little espresso, and waited. I didn't really know what I was waiting for, but it better be good.

It was about twenty minutes later, and I was into my second espresso and my first cigar of the new day, when the phones rang. It was a little too soon to be McGovern and a little too late to be the call that was going to change my life.

On about the fifth ring I picked up the blower on the left and listened to Ratso's rodentlike voice loudly repeating the word "Kinkstah!"

I took a patient puff on the cigar and waited. In time, I was rewarded.

"I've got something for you, Kinkstah."

"Lay it on me, Ratman."

He did.

According to Ratso, 88 stood for the eighth letter of the alphabet, H, repeated once. As in, he said, *Heil* Hitler. Certain organizations and corporations took the code name after the fall of the Third Reich. The Nazi version of "Save your Confederate money, boys, the South will rise again." Only these guys *believed* it.

While this revelation didn't really surprise me, it didn't do my nerves much good. Apparently, we were dealing with whom I thought we were dealing with.

Unpleasant.

"Oh, Sherlock," Ratso said, "I uncovered something else pretty interesting that you might want to know. It involves the Austrians prior to the time of the *Anschluss,* the German invasion that really wasn't an invasion because the Austrians welcomed the Nazis with open arms.

"Apparently, each Austrian political party had its own flower symbol. The atheists wore pansies. The socialists wore red carnations. And—get this—the Austrian Nazis wore a blue cornflower in their lapels."

"Interesting," I said. "I wonder if that helps explain why so many Austrians today suffer from Waldheimer's Disease?"

"What's Waldheimer's Disease?"

"It's when you can't remember that you used to be a Nazi."

27

I sipped a luke espresso and gazed at New York from the kitchen window. A wall, a billboard, a fire escape. What else did you need? They ought to put it on the back of a postcard, so I could send one to my Aunt Rhoda in Pocatello. But Aunt Rhoda wants the Empire State Building. Aunt Rhoda wants the Statue of Liberty. Aunt Rhoda wants the Staten Island Ferry. That's why she lives in Pocatello.

The more I looked out the window, the more I was convinced that this was a classic view of the city. It was undeniably New York; it just wasn't postcard material.

I thought of the postcards that the government of Borneo had issued. Borneo is the only place in the world where tribes of people live communally in longhouses. These majestic, rustic structures, built high on stilts and stretching across a city block of jungle, have never been deemed worthy of postcard status. Nor would the Borneo government ever approve a postcard of a four-foot-tall Punan tribesman holding a seven-foot-long blowpipe. The postcards of Borneo I'd seen had mostly been of things like a new two-story office building in Kuching, the capital city. No doubt the government was very proud of the office building, but what would Aunt Rhoda think?

I stared out the window into a certain middle distance of the heart, and I felt a numbing loneliness invade my spirit. There were a lot of things they didn't put on postcards. Like a blond girl in a peach-colored dress driving a little white T-bird convertible down a dusty country road. A large white standard poodle named Leo is sitting in the seat beside her. They're listening to country music on the car radio. The sun is shining on the girl's hair, and she's smiling a lovely crooked smile that makes her look a little like Hank Williams. Wish you were here.

I walked away from the window, wandered over to the desk, sat down, and watched the phones for a while. Waiting for McGovern to call was about as tedious as waiting for Godot, though not, very possibly, as existential an experience.

I fed the cat. That was existential enough for a Thursday morning.

I thought about what Ratso had told me earlier concerning the meaning of the name 88 and the blue cornflower business. Ratso and I had also agreed that my having a little chat with Carmen was in order for that evening. I preferred to have the little chat without the presence of a large rat, but I realized that Ratso now too had a special interest in the case. Ratso and I were not the most objective, scientific practitioners of crime-solving under the best of circumstances. I wondered openly about our abilities to solve crimes against humanity.

At around six-thirty, with a rather fitful power nap under my belt, I left the cat in charge, grabbed a few cigars for the road, and started to leave for the Spanish Inquisition.

I had just turned the doorknob to the right when the phones rang. I returned to the desk, picked up the blower on the left, and listened grimly.

Godot had arrived.

28

Vandam Street looked dark and spectral as I made my way to Ratso's place that evening, and my own troubled thoughts mirrored the foreboding ambience of the street. After hearing what McGovern had to say about last night's twin killing in Bayonne, I was convinced beyond a shadow of a doubt that Bob Dylan and Jesus Christ were out of it. And I didn't particularly want to invite home to dinner what was left.

According to McGovern, the two component parts of the radioactive crab, heretofore known as Goldilocks and Gorgeous George, had other names and other games. They were widely known in the New York–New Jersey area as neo-Nazis.

They did not look like neo-Nazis, black yachtsmen, or anything else I'd known in the past. Rambam had once introduced me to a group of neo-Nazis several weeks before he'd visited upon them an event that has since become known as "the Invasion of the Killer Jews." But Rambam's neo-Nazis had looked more like what you'd expect neo-Nazis to look like. Prison tans, tattoos everywhere, axle grease from the local body shop under their fingernails. They hadn't looked like the kind of guys who'd need to cut the labels out of their fine Italian jackets.

Of course, I reflected as I crossed Seventh Avenue against the light, you can't judge a book by its cover. Especially once they've burned the book.

But by far the most interesting piece of information that McGovern was able to unearth was the means by

which our charming blond friends had been delivered into
the hands of Charon, the ferryboatman of Hell. They had
been injected with a little-known pesticide called phenoxylcholine.

Now that I thought about it, the Nazis always had been
great ones when it came to injections. I remembered the
account I'd once read of the German office worker who had
recalled that groups of Gypsy children from local orphan-
ages had been taken up the stairway to a room one floor
above him in the same building. In that room, good German doctors would inject water, air, gasoline, or toxic
chemicals into the veins of the children. The substances
would circulate briefly in the veins until they reached the
heart, at which point the child would drop dead on the
floor. At regular intervals of about sixty seconds the German office worker and his innocuous, bespectacled colleagues would hear the sound of the body of a small child
hitting the floor directly above them. They had, so they
later contended, no way of knowing what was going on up
there. Of course, over periods of some months, groups of
children had been led up the stairs, and none of them ever
were seen to come down again. But who could tell?

It must also be reported, to the credit of the peculiar,
meticulous nature of the German people, that there was no
work stoppage among the office workers. Their work, it is
gratifying to note, did not suffer like the children.

The more I thought about the sounds of small children
dropping dead, the less I was starting to mind Winnie
Katz's lesbian dance class.

As I walked up Prince Street toward Ratso's apartment,
I leaned into a chill wind and remembered the last mor-
sel that McGovern had come up with. The coroner's lab
had run an analysis of the substance that had eighty-sixed
Goldilocks and Gorgeous George and subsequently seeped
into their Aryan entrails. Phenoxylcholine, according to

McGovern, was a fairly archaic derivative of Zyklon-B, the chemical the Nazis had used in the gas chambers.

I had to admit one thing. McGovern was a hell of a leg man.

Impressions can often be misleading. My friend Sammy Allred from Austin, Texas, once told me about the time he met a lady who was walking a duck on a leash. "Where you goin' with that pig?" Sammy asked. "That's no pig, stupid," she said. "It's a duck." "I was talking to the duck," Sammy said.

I didn't know who the hell or what the hell Carmen Cohen was but I was sure the hell going to find out.

Even though she was no longer wearing lace panties or hanging by her wrists from a clothes rod in a closet of the Pierre Hotel, she still managed to look good. You didn't need a sniperscope to see that the broad had a lot of class. Too much class for Ratso, I thought. I'd known outcall masseuses with more class than Ratso.

But I wasn't here to compile information for the Social Register. I was here to try to unravel what had become a rather unpleasant ball of yarn, and I was beginning to wonder what kind of yarn I was going to get from Carmen Cohen.

It didn't take long to find out. Ratso offered me a seat beside him on the sofa with the skid marks on it.

"No thanks," I said. "I'll pace."

Carmen was sitting in a straight-backed chair looking

beautiful, sulky, magical, and secretive, like a Gypsy child that the Germans had missed. With only a little goading from me, she launched into her story. It was pretty straightforward as far as it went. There were, however, a few distractions. One was Carmen crossing her legs about eleven times during the narrative. She was wearing a short black leather skirt and long, lovely Latin wheels.

Two was Carmen's pronunciation of the letter *J* like *Y*, so the word "jungle" sounded like "yungle." But this could be overlooked and probably usually was, since it had to contend with distraction number one. I sat down on the couch a little to the north of the skid marks, to listen and to observe.

Carmen's parents had died in a plane crash when she was an infant. She was adopted by a wealthy plantation owner who'd come to Argentina from Europe, where he'd been an engineer of some sort. Sometime in her early teens, Carmen's adoptive parents were divorced, an event that apparently was quite traumatic for her, because she went on about it for some little time.

"Let's just operate on the assumption," I said, perhaps a bit unkindly, "that everybody comes from a broken home."

Ratso gave me a stern look. Carmen, however, appeared unfazed, and continued with her narrative.

She'd met John Morgan about three years ago, when she was only eighteen years old. They saw each other only sporadically for a while, and then, about a year ago, they started to dance pretty close and Carmen brought John home to meet her father.

At first the two men seemed to get along very well. Then something, which Carmen appeared to be rather vague about, happened to poison the waters between Morgan and her father. I pressed Carmen on the point. She maintained she'd never understood what had caused the breach between them. Ratso watched her intently. I lit a cigar and studied her black eyes through a wreath of blue smoke. She was something, all right.

"It's just as if they've disappeared into the yungle," she said, crossing her legs for the twelfth time. Who was counting?

"Hold the weddin'," I said. "We know John's missing in action, but who *else* has disappeared recently?"

"My father," she said.

"She may be dreideling us, Ratso," I said, as he accompanied me down in an elevator that was at least big enough for several anorectic midgets.

Ratso stared at me in disbelief. "C'mon, Kinkster," he said. "She's been under a great strain lately. You heard what she said. She comes home six days ago. Her father's gone. The place is completely trashed. The only thing missing in the house is a picture of her and John Morgan that she kept on the bureau in her bedroom."

"And now Morgan himself seems to have disappeared. Maybe they both just vanished into the yungle."

"That's cute. Leave her alone for a while. She's had a bad shock."

The hallway to the street in Ratso's building always smelled faintly like urine because Ratso had a pet bum who slept there on cold nights. I lit a cigar as we walked briskly through to the street.

"Oh, she seems to be holding up all right," I said. "I'm more worried about the two of us."

"That's very self-directed, Kinkstah," Ratso said as he *goniffed* a papaya from the Moonie fruit stand on the corner.

"As Hillel said, 'If I am not for myself, who will be for me?'"

"Yeah," said Ratso, taking an unnecessarily large bite of papaya, "but can you say that while you're standing on one foot?"

"Of course, but it'd be hard getting home that way."

It wasn't that I didn't want to believe Carmen's story. I was ready to believe "The Princess and the Pea," if it would help me find out what had happened to John Morgan. It was just that all the loose ends in this affair were beginning to flay me to death. Had Morgan been in New York recently? The guy who'd developed the film thought so. And what was it about those photographs that kept nagging me like a mosquito that had slipped under the net?

Why would someone employ infamous Nazi methodology to whack a couple neo-Nazis? Could this increasingly grotesque puzzle reach back almost fifty years in time and across the length and breadth of three continents? As my friend and personal guru Earl Buckelew always says back in Texas, "It'll all come out in the wash if you use enough Tide." All too often, however, there is not enough tide in the affairs of men.

"One point that was interesting," I said to Ratso, "was Carmen's comment about John always flying off to Hong Kong. Hong Kong was the hub city en route to Borneo when I went there twenty years ago. I'll bet Borneo was his destination. Now why was he flying back and forth so often, and who was paying for all his travel and accommodations?"

Ratso shrugged and pitched the papaya over his shoulder onto a shiny Porsche parked in front of a wine bar. I didn't like wine bars, and I didn't like Porches much, either. Papayas were all right.

"It looks," I said, "like an extremely unpleasant version of the ol' grasshopper game."

"Yeah," said Ratso. "The ol' grasshopper game." He turned and started back toward his apartment. A moment later he stopped, turned around again, and shouted, "What's the ol' grasshopper game?"

I took a last puff on the cigar and killed it in the gutter of Mulberry Street not terribly far from where Joey Gallo got his.

"In due course, Watson," I said.

It's always a mistake to be walking along minding your own business in New York. It's the kind of irrational, bizarre behavioral error that seems to make trouble jump out at you from the hand shadow of a duck. Yet, though it might've appeared that way, minding my own business wasn't exactly what I was doing that night.

I was looking into Carmen's eyes. I could see them almost as an after-image against the hepatitis yellow of the occasional street lamp. They stared seductively at me from behind the bars of first-floor windows. And what was particularly worrisome about them was that they seemed to be telling me something that Carmen had not.

I had shown Carmen the photographs. There had been a noticeable reaction only to two of them. One was the picture of John Morgan in the Land Rover with his hair gently disheveled by the wind and his green eyes shining like a rain forest at dawn. She'd lingered lovingly over that one.

The second photograph that seemed to stop her momentarily was the one of the two old men in the jungle. They were pretty ancient geezers, both wearing panama hats and smiling, and one of them, as I remembered, had a space between his two front teeth, which was better, I supposed, than having a space between your ears. Other than that, there was nothing remarkable about the photo aside from Carmen's reaction to it—a sudden intake of breath before she caught herself.

"Who are those men?" I'd asked her.

"I don't know," she'd said, but she'd looked confused. She said she'd seen a picture of one of them before—the one with the little space between his teeth—at John's apartment in Buenos Aires. When she'd asked him who the man was, he'd said, "Dr. Breitenbach, I presume."

"Dr. Breitenbach, I presume," I muttered to myself as I headed down Vandam Street in the darkness. That told me exactly nothing. But it did sound like Morgan. Enigmatic, playful right to the end. But *was* this the end? Was Morgan really dead, or, as we say in New York, was he just currently not working on a project?

I wondered. But I didn't wonder long.

Five bald-headed geeks had surrounded me. Like malevolent walking cue balls, they slouched languidly, expressionlessly forward in the queasy manner of enemy Martian plants. The light from a distant street lamp gleamed wickedly off their hairless cue-ball craniums. Nobody smiled.

In their small eyes I recognized that their fervent dream was to rack my soul.

31

Skinheads are neo-Nazi groups springing up in America almost as fast as BMW dealerships in southern California. Skinheads hate blacks and Jews, and they don't bother to take into consideration the fact that most Jews and blacks don't even like each other very much.

Cops'll tell you that it's easier to stop a pit-bull attack or a runaway locomotive than to deal with a gathering of skinheads. The reason is because skinheads have no neurons. The casual stick in the eye does not usually faze them. Cutting off their legs just below the knees rarely impedes their forward progress. This is because, from almost any human standpoint, they are dead before they shave their heads.

Things weren't looking too good for me, either. I was standing on a dark, deserted sidewalk in New York City, a block and a half from my loft, like a human wagon train encircled by pale engines of hate. They looked like five aging heavy-metal sidemen with no words and no music. Negative stage charisma.

I remember I was staring at a picture of an eagle on the T-shirt of one guy. It was not an American-looking eagle. Something in its eye told me that it had been an engineering major, and that it wished very much to land upon the bridge of my nose. It was some kind of kraut eagle, I remember thinking.

I was staring transfixedly at the eagle like a large urban field mouse when a searing pain shot suddenly through both of my eyes. I wheeled blindly to the left, leveled a savage kick with my cowboy boot about *huevos*-high, and connected with nothing but the hatred in the air. My eyes cleared enough to notice the metal-stud bracelets the skinheads were wearing. Somebody had slipped around behind me and rasped me across the eyes.

What little I knew about defending yourself single-handedly against a gang I'd picked up from Boris Shapiro's Berlitz combat karate class, from a few tough local micks I knew, and from several friendly individuals in the Jewish Defense League. The situations, however, had always been hypothetical. This one, unfortunately, wasn't. Like so many other aspects of life, the wheels tend to come off when things get nonhypothetical. Only if you're lucky do you live to hypothesize another day. Hypothetically speaking, of course.

I backed up against a brick wall, thereby preventing them from completely surrounding me. The next thing to do, I knew, was to find the leader and do something unpleasant to him if possible, like pulling one of his eyeballs out of its socket. You can usually tell the gang leader, because he's the one doing the most yapping. But it was impossible to make this determination, because all five were ominously silent. Furthermore, they had the same shaved domes and the same dreadful glazed, hate-riddled, halibut eyes. They advanced slowly, then stopped, almost as though they were operating under a hive or swarm instinct. It was as if five dead people were playing games with you.

I decided to go for the guy with the eagle on his chest, but just as this thought struck me, something else did, too. It was a heavy chain that slammed down across the top of my head and flattened my left ear like a silver-dollar pancake. Another chain zinged me heavily on the back of the neck and knocked me to the sidewalk.

I felt hot pain mingling with cold fear. The two sensations seemed to alternate rapidly, kind of like taking a hotel shower in Mexico. Before I could get back on my feet, I took a black leather boot to the head and one to the solar plexus. Fear went quietly to the back burner. Pain was all I felt. Rough hands, boots, chains, and studded bracelets rained down on me. I tried futilely several times to blink the blood out of my eyes, and then gave it up for Lent.

The pain was now gone. A peculiar and almost peaceful numbness had set in, and I recognized that it was almost time for me to say *adiós* to mañanaland. I could see nothing but blurred images, but I was hearing a new sound—a sickening thudding sound that I assumed was my skull giving way. I could feel very little by now, but the noise was very clear. It sounded like *klaang, klaang, klaang.* Somewhere in the deep recesses of what was left of my brain I remembered that a *klaang* was a canal in Thailand. They don't always come in handy, but it's nice to know these things.

I listened now—which was about all I could do—and I heard it again distinctly. *Klaang, klaang.* Then a hand was on my shoulder and a voice was saying, "Hey, man, that was a close one. I was waitin' for you on your fire escape, and I saw this going down and rushed over. Just in time, it looks like."

The hand was now mopping the blood from my eyes with a handkerchief. I blinked a few times and saw Zev standing over me with a blood-soaked handkerchief in one hand and a lead pipe in the other. Four skinheads were gone, and one was sprawled appropriately in the gutter.

Zev was a mysterious friend of mine who'd been rumored to have fought with the Israeli Army in Lebanon and with the Mujahedeen against the Russians in Afghanistan. For many enemies of democracy, Zev had been the last vision they'd seen on earth, and, fortunately for me, he also went in for *klaanging* skinheads.

"Jesus Christ, Zev," I said in a slurred and subdued voice, "you saved my life."

Zev laughed. "*Azoy!*" he shouted.

"What the hell does that mean?"

"Freely translated?"

"Whatever gets you through the night," I said as he slowly helped me to my feet.

"It's Jewish. Not Hebrew. Jewish."

"Jewish," I repeated.

"Freely translated, it means: 'We beat the shit out of them.' "

Unfortunately, I was busy counting my kneecaps and was not fully able to savor our victory. I felt like the other guy you should've seen. I was weaker than prime-time programming.

"Zev," I said, "check that guy in the gutter for papers or identification, will you?" Zev went over to the guy and I started to stumble slowly in the direction of the loft.

"He's clean," Zev said.

I'd taken about three more steps when I heard Zev speak again.

"He's also dead," he said.

We did a Jim Rockford.

Within minutes I was back in the loft lying on the sofa, chewing a green substance called *gat* that Zev had given me. *Gat* is a cloverlike plant that, according to Zev, kills pain, makes you high, and is only chewed by Yemenite Jews. I wasn't a Yemenite Jew, but I was beginning to feel like one.

The cat was watching me anxiously from the rocking chair. Zev was looking down on me with concern in his eyes. I was a lot farther away from New York than Westchester.

"That *gat*'s good stuff," said Zev. "You know, in Israel it's actually illegal for anyone except Yemenite Jews to chew it."

"That's why I love America," I said.

By midnight my body had settled down to a dull throb. Zev, apparently, had been taking Ratso lessons. He announced his intention, as Ratso had done several times in the past, to stay with me in the loft until I recovered from my little accident. I was fond of Zev and rather grudgingly grateful to him for saving my life, but I didn't want the guy to put down roots. The cat and I had a fairly high-maintenance relationship as it was.

"You're going to be all right," said Zev. "Just don't look in the mirror for a couple of days."

"I look that bad?"

"Worse."

"It's a good thing," I said, "that I'm not an escort in the Miss Mean-minded Vacuous Bitch Pageant."

I got Zev to rev up the espresso machine, and, miraculously, I found an only slightly crushed cigar in one of the little pockets of my hunting vest where some Americans keep their shotgun shells. I sat up slowly and painfully and began the prenuptial arrangements on the cigar. Sometimes it's good to have something to do with your hands. I lit the cigar, always keeping it slightly above the flame.

Zev brought over two cups of espresso, handed me one, and sat down on the couch. "I'll stay tonight," he said. "In case those guys try to come back."

"One of them won't," I said grimly. I took a puff on the cigar. Zev laughed. It was a high-pitched, peculiar, dangerous sound. I took a sip of the espresso, swished it around with the *gat*, and swallowed hard. "Not bad," I said. Of course, anything with *gat* wasn't bad.

Zev chuckled. The chuckle was worse than the laugh. "Zev," I said, "let me play psychologist for a moment." You don't want to be a psychologist for much longer than that. You might find out something you don't want to know.

"Let me ask you a question. A guy got spliced tonight, right?"

"Right."

I know he probably tied his shoes with little Nazis, but how does it make you feel?" I took an insightful, other-directed puff on the cigar. The smoke, as usual, was also other-directed.

"How does it make me feel? I'll tell you how it makes me feel." He got up and walked over to the window. He looked out into the darkness and raised a clenched fist in the air. "Nazis—six million," he shouted, "Jews—one!"

"Yeah," I said to the cat, "but who's keeping score?"

It was a few moments after that that I reached into the inside pocket of my hunting vest and realized that John Morgan's photographs were missing.

Sometimes you can see things more clearly when they're not there. Most of the great books about human freedom, for instance, were written in prison. From my own personal experience, I have put a black pill of opium into a cup of coffee, drunk it down, stood at the edge of the Borneo jungle staring out across the South China Sea, and seen America more lucidly than at any time in my life. This was made possible partly by the drug, but mostly, I believe, by the physical absence of America.

Following this somewhat distorted but more often than not accurate line of thinking, one might conclude that a man who professes to be searching for a white tiger in the jungle might well be searching for something else.

It was Friday afternoon. Zev had gone back to Brooklyn. I was sitting at my desk with a fresh cigar and a twelve-year-old bottle of Jameson, not looking at photographs and not looking in the mirror. Life, I always say, is what happens when you're not looking.

I poured and killed a shot. Then I took a few puffs on the cigar, closed my eyes, leaned back in the chair, and tried to visualize the photographs that were no longer in my possession. The images ran by like a slide carousel slowly spinning in my brain. A tributary, I supposed, of the Amazon River cutting through the jungle, here and there vaguely reflecting the sky . . . prehistoric trees bearing strange fruit you never see in shopping carts . . . branches brown and gnarled hanging timelessly in the clouds . . . a little highway heading nowhere, sparsely traveled, lighted by the sun . . . a Land Rover pulled off to the left side of the road . . . a bus going by on the right, full of people and chickens and bananas . . . John Morgan's face smiling recklessly into forever . . .

I found it hard to accept that this man could be dead. I held the picture of John in my head and attempted to adjust the focus.

When I did, I realized that something was very wrong with the picture. I'd assumed the little blurs of people on the bus to be South American Indians, peasants, farmers, but now I wasn't so sure. When you're not looking at pictures, you cannot look again and again and sometimes memory will triumph over imagination. Many tribes of people across the globe bear distinct physical resemblances to each other. That was one of the reasons I gave the shrink for not wanting to go fight in Vietnam when my Peace Corps service was completed. After working two-and-a-half years in the Far East, I didn't want to go back and kill the same people wearing the same funny pointed hats. I conjured up the passengers on the bus again and realized they could've been anybody.

Then I noted the direction the bus was heading. Then I backed up one frame and noticed the direction John was going in the Land Rover. Then I opened my eyes and saw that I'd been a world away from the truth.

34

"You see," I said to the cat, "unless I'm very much mistaken, there was almost no British influence in Latin America." The cat scratched her left ear rather irritably with her left rear paw.

"All right, there's the Falkland Islands, I'll grant you that. But what else have you got? British Honduras is now only a stamp." The cat looked at me and blinked her eyes rather sleepily. The cat had never been much of a philatelist.

"You can see what the problem is, can't you?" The cat shook her head violently. Either there was a flea in her ear, or she couldn't see what the problem was.

I almost hadn't seen it myself.

I had met John Morgan in Borneo, so it was to Borneo that I'd originally looked for possible clues to his mysterious background. But from Carmen's statements and from the increasingly unpleasant Nazi undercurrents in the case, I'd assumed that whatever he'd been up to recently had been based in South America. Now I saw that the photographs—even in their absence—proved this thesis to be wrong.

Normal people, I thought, drive on the right-hand side of the road. Only where there's been early and pervasive British influence do they drive on the left. But John, to my knowledge, had never been to India or Africa. And couldn't have been driving on the left anywhere in South America. The only jungle terrain in the world with British driving patterns that could logically match the photograph was Borneo.

So the photographs were from Borneo.

The hornbill feather I'd found in the long-dead lawyer's office was from Borneo.

Therefore, whatever nefarious schemes Morgan had recently been involved in had transpired in Borneo. I poured a hefty jolt into the bull's horn and downed it with a shudder.

"So Morgan *had* been searching for a white tiger," I said to the cat. I puffed a bit on the cigar and ran down the peculiar convoluted affair in my mind for a few moments.

"And I'll bet you a case of Jameson against a case of tuna that that tiger has blue eyes."

Weekends and holidays, I've always thought, are strictly for amateurs. Time for some middle-level German civil servants of all nationalities to adjust their wire-rimmed spectacles and go out and be party animals. I didn't have any wire-rimmed glasses, so I stayed home Friday night. Also, my face was turning a nice purple hue, and I was beginning to feel like the hunchback of New York, so I figured I'd hang around with the cat. The cat didn't seem to mind, though I did catch her looking rather furtively at me a few times. Probably my imagination.

One thing that I definitely knew wasn't in my imagination was the fact that somebody'd set those skinheads on me. Either someone had been watching the loft and tailed me that evening, or somebody'd set me up. And there weren't very many somebodies who knew I was going over to Ratso's that night. I didn't much like where things seemed to be pointing.

Of course, I didn't much like a lot of things, and I would very probably continue not liking a lot of things until the big iron crab grabbed me and they put me in the ground. There was nothing I could do about it. It was part of being an adult. Part of being an American. Part of being. It was life on the Mississippi.

Saturday morning I did not go to the Fun Club to see Tom Mix. I stayed in the loft, chewed a little *gat,* and chewed a little fat with the cat. If you were stationed in the *ulu* and you ever told that many rhymes to anyone in the Peace Corps brass, or you didn't come out of your house for a few days, they'd send in a helicopter factory-equipped with a shrink to pluck you out of there and take you to wig city for observation. I'd seen it happen any number of times. It wasn't *Apocalypse Now;* it was simply that in the *ulu* you became adept at hearing a twig snap, and the Peace Corps brass became adept at hearing a wig snap. That was one reason I rarely spoke to Peace Corps officials the whole time I was in Borneo. Now, rather unfortunately, it crossed my desk that it was mandatory for me to break that silence.

That afternoon I called John Mapes, an old Peace Corps buddy of mine who was currently residing in Hawaii. There were a lot of good reasons to currently reside in Hawaii, and one of them was that characters with blue cornflowers in their lapels didn't follow you around hotel lobbies.

Mapes, who was rather widely known as the barefoot economist for the state of Hawaii, sounded a bit grumpy. The reason, I quickly divined, was the five-hour time difference between New York and Hawaii. It was 7:15 Saturday morning in Hawaii. But in New York, unfortunately, it was past time for me to get my ass in gear. After Mapes

had had time to become a little more coherent and civil, I
filled him in on the John Morgan situation and, in return,
got nothing but perplexing questions. Mapes knew less
than I did about Morgan's activities in recent years. He did,
however, still have some connection with official Peace
Corpsdom in Washington, he said.

"You could call Norman Potts," he said. "Remember,
he used to be country director. Now he's got some cushy
desk job in Washington. Of course, he hates your guts."

"Yeah, Mapes, but as Gandhi said, 'Forgiveness is the
ornament of the brave.' Surely he's forgotten by now."

Mapes laughed. "In your case, pal, not a chance."

There were many fine people, I was sure, who worked
for the Peace Corps in Washington. It was just my luck that
the only one I knew was Norman Potts. He never had
adored me, but it came as something of a shock that, after
twenty years, the guy still wanted to see me in hell. Potts,
I remembered, had had me forcibly "returned to my own
culture" after two-and-a-half years in the jungle. That, in
military terms, was not as ignominious as a dishonorable
discharge, but it wasn't exactly the Distinguished Flying
Cross. I'd never forgiven him for it, and apparently he'd
never forgiven me for whatever it was that he'd never
forgiven me for. By this time I'd forgotten. In twenty years
you meet a lot of new people that you can piss off, and you
forget just what it was that fired some pompous stuffed
shirt's rocket somewhere in the distant mists of the past. At
least I hadn't lost my touch.

I talked a little longer to Mapes, then I wheedled Potts's
office phone number out of him, said good-bye and rang off.
I hadn't seen Mapes in twenty years, but there's always
some kind of bond forged between two people who are
caught in a monsoon together for several months. I remembered when I'd left Borneo, Mapes had put me aboard a
freighter for Singapore. I was shivering with a malarial
fever, pale as a spinning ghost, weighed about twenty-

seven pounds, and didn't know where the hell I was going or why. Otherwise, I was fine.

The tropics will do that to you. I remember Mapes kissing me good-bye as he put me on the boat. Like he knew he'd never see me again. There was deep generosity and kindness in the man, and there was something very close to pity in his eyes. Now that I think about it.

Sunday passed in a blur about as vague as Jesus' face on the Shroud of Turin. I didn't go to church, I didn't have a Sunday dinner with the whole family, and I didn't give a damn. I was a pagan like Breaker Morant.

By Sunday night I'd spoken to Ratso and explained to him the significance of a Land Rover's driving on the left-hand side of the road through the jungle. He was dutifully impressed.

"What now, Kinkster?" he'd wanted to know.

"Well, we can't very well hop a plane for Borneo, can we?"

"Not till we find out if the Rangers get into the play-offs."

Like I said, he was dutifully impressed.

Sunday night I also got a call from Rambam. He'd done some work on the John Morgan case, he said. It was imperative that the two of us return to New Jersey Monday morning. After some little protestations on my part, it was agreed that he'd pick me up at eleven and tell me the details at that time. He didn't want to talk over the phone. I told him I didn't know why. If the telephone was good enough for J. Edgar Hoover, it was good enough for me. He hung up.

As I lay in bed that night with the cat and a terminal case of insomnia, I plotted the approach I'd use on Norman Potts in the morning. If I could get hold of an actual Peace Corps file, it would go a long way toward at least clearing up the question of who was John Morgan. Once I got that taken care of, I could worry about the Nazis under the bed.

Several of those spectral creatures, unfortunately, seemed to have slithered out of late, and were more than a little determined, apparently, to link their foggy-nighted, kerosene-blooded, ringless-fingered karma with that of my own.

"This is Mike McGovern," I said, "with the *New York Daily News.*" I took a sip of espresso and winked at the cat. It was Monday morning and I was on the blower to the Peace Corps Administrative Offices in our nation's capital.

"Norman Potts here," said the voice on the blower. "What can I do for you?" There were a few things Norman could do for me, but if I told him what they were, I'd never find out about John Morgan.

"We're doing a follow-up feature for our Sunday magazine on Peace Corps volunteers who've returned to the States. Jay Maeder, the editor, says he wants a 'Twenty Years Later—Where Are They Now?' sort of thing, and I'd—"

"RPCVs," said Norman Potts.

"I beg your pardon?"

"Returned Peace Corps Volunteers," he said with just a hint of irritation. "We call them RPCVs."

"That's good. We'll use that." I took another sip of espresso and rolled my eyes in the direction of the lesbian dance class. "I'd just like to ask you a few questions."

"Shoot," said Norman Potts. He was just one of the guys.

"As I told your secretary, we're highlighting one particular, uh, RPCV. He's now a Wall Street success story, but we'd like some bio information and a photo of him from the sixties when he still had dreams in his eyes. His name is John Morgan, and he was stationed in Sarawak, which I located on my map and found to be in Borneo. What we need—"

"That's very curious."

"Not really. We chose Morgan at random. We just—"

"Not what I'm talking about. Someone called us last week wanting information on John Morgan. Now, when you get two calls concerning one individual in twenty years and they both come within a week of each other, it's rather curious, if you see what I mean."

I saw what he meant.

"Who was the other caller?"

"Fellow from some European publishing consortium. A West German magazine was doing a retrospective article. 'Peaceful alternatives to the Vietnam War.' Something like that. Wanted to see the Peace Corps file on John Morgan, a volunteer in Borneo, they said. We don't release files to the press or the public, Mr. McGovern. This has always been our policy. You can understand this, I'm sure."

I understood and lit a cigar at the same time. "Quite sensible," I said. "What did you do? Did you give the caller the information?" If it was the same Norman Potts, all you had to do was wind him up and let him go.

"No. He was very insistent, and I didn't like his attitude. A lot of the volunteers I remember, but this one I didn't. So when he hung up, I checked all the Borneo groups and found **no** John Morgan. It was rather perplexing, as you can imagine."

I could imagine. I took a puff on the cigar and imagined quite a lot of things, none of them very pleasant.

"We call this a 'news leak,' Mr. Potts. No doubt emanating from our tabloid competition here in the city. They'll stoop to anything to beat us to a story, and I'm afraid it's created somewhat of a nuisance for you. It's one of the things the Fourth Estate is not particularly proud of."

"Actually, it made me curious, so I popped John Morgan into the big computer and found he *was indeed* a volunteer at one time. But it was earlier than they'd thought, and it wasn't in Borneo. It was Argentina. 1963."

"Interesting," I said. "Did the caller say who he was or where he was calling from?"

"Said his name was Harvey Pickelner. He was based out of some town in New Jersey."

"Bayonne ring any bells?"

"That's it. Bayonne. How'd you know that?"

"We've had trouble there before."

Something ugly was happening, and it was happening on a lot of levels. People who were knocked off, like Goldilocks, Gorgeous George, and the anonymous skinhead, seemed to be being quickly replaced, like worn-out parts of a much larger machine, for a much larger purpose. Good German engineering.

I got some bio information on Morgan from Potts that didn't tell me much. But, much more significantly, he agreed to release a photo of Morgan to my "stringer" in Washington. The photo, I figured, ought to tell me something.

Twenty years, I noticed, had done little to leaven the cool, cautious, slightly bored, bureaucratic inflections in Potts's voice. Even so, this was the longest, and certainly the pleasantest, conversation I'd ever had with him. Of course, he thought I was Mike McGovern, but you couldn't hold that against him.

"Are you interested in the other volunteer they wanted to know about?" asked Potts. "*Him* I remember very well, unfortunately. *Very* unpleasant fellow. Couldn't deal with authority at all."

"We've got a few of those right here at the National Desk." I made an attempt at a hearty, McGovernlike laugh.

"Not like this one," said Potts. "He thought he was

Lord Jim out there in the jungle. Practically destroyed our working relationship with the host country. No, I'm not likely to forget him."

I took a slightly paranoid pull on the cigar.

I waited.

"Guy named Friedman," said Norman Potts.

I exhaled.

My "stringer" in Washington was a Lebanese Druse rock-'n'-roll guitarist named Jimmie Silman, who preferred to be known, cosmically enough, as Ratso. I spoke of him sometimes as Washington Ratso to differentiate him from the New York Ratso, but when I spoke to him I just called him Ratso. I was a two-Ratso man.

Why two adult white male Americans would wish to be known as Ratso in the first place was a mystery to me, but I went along with it. Ratso, I always figured, was a pretty funny name for someone to have, much less two people. Of course, if you stopped to think about it, Kinky was a funny name, too.

While waiting for Rambam to show up, I moved smoothly into my second and third espressos, thought about—but decided against—breaking out cigar number two of the morning, and lined up things with Washington Ratso. Washington Ratso had never been a stringer for the *New York Daily News* before, and he was rather excited about it. How is a journalist supposed to act? he wanted to know. I told him that a journalist acts just about like a rock-'n'-roll guitarist except that he should dress a little tackier. Ratso didn't think that would present any problem, said he was between gigs right now anyway, and pledged to personally messenger the alleged photo of John Morgan to me within the next forty-seven hours. I gave him my standard line about time being the money of love and told him to get crackin'. Big-time journalism was tough work, and it was starting to wear me out.

I stood at the kitchen window juggling the puppet head nervously and waiting for Rambam. It was really too much, I thought, to ask somebody to go to New Jersey twice in the same lifetime. Well, we'd work things out when Rambam arrived.

It was a cloudy morning, cold and bleak, with the wind whipping through the rusty slats in the fire escapes. The scenery looked pretty much the color of the lining of your lungs. The only green that met the eye was inside the loft: the houseplants left by the Greek woman I subletted from, who looked like a spider. Every once in a while I'd water the plants or spit a little Jameson on them. At the moment they were thriving better than I was. In fact, they seemed kind of smug. Where in the hell was Rambam?

I put the puppet head back on top of the refrigerator, walked over to the desk, took cigar number two out of Sherlock Holmes's head, set it in the guillotine, lopped off its butt, leaned back in the chair, set fire to the end of it, and took a relaxed puff just as Rambam's voice carried its coarse Brooklyn obscenities through my Manhattan windowpane.

I did not move from the chair.

I haven't seen any studies on the subject from any pointy-headed university professors, but it's my contention that cigar smokers live longer than the average nonsmoker. This is because of our attitude toward life. We don't let people screaming for puppet heads ruffle our feathers too much. Especially when they're not very punctual and they want to go to New Jersey. This is why most cigar smokers live longer than they want to. They also live longer than anyone else wants them to.

Eventually, Rambam entered the door of the loft with the puppet head in one hand and a brown envelope in the other. "Jesus Christ," he said. "What happened to your face?"

"Nothing," I said. "It was just a little hunting accident in Peru."

"Better tell Mother Rambam all about it," he said, flipping me the puppet head. I walked over and put it on top of the refrigerator and came back and sat at the desk, where Rambam had already pulled up a chair.

I told him the whole saga of the skinheads. I started with the interview with Carmen, my leaving Ratso's place, and my strong suspicions that someone had set the skinheads on me. Rambam listened in silence. When I came to the part about Zev, he laughed and shook his head.

"What's the matter?" I asked.

"Nothing. I'm just glad the little bastard's on our side."

By the time I finished with the account of the dead skinhead, Rambam was baring his teeth at me in a rather frightening smile.

"What the hell are you smiling about?" I asked.

"I'm just thinking of how much fun we're gonna have," he said, "when we finally catch up with these baddies."

"Yeah," I said rather doubtfully, as I felt the large, painful, purple swelling under my left eye, "that *will* be fun."

38

Rambam and possibly even Zev, I reflected as Rambam nosed the Jag out of the Holland Tunnel and onto the New Jersey Turnpike, were probably not clinically ill. They were, however, a little out of line with the other ducks. I'd seen Rambam with my own eyes waste half a dozen hired gunman from two warring Colombian cocaine cartels, and the stories about Zev were legend. Zev walking home at two in the morning on the tops of parked cars. Zev allowing himself to be dragged up the stairs of the Lone Star Cafe by the hair. (Thereby demonstrating the strength of his hair. Of course, he was monstered on slivovitz at the time.) Zev delivering things like diamonds and silencers to places even Negroes feared to tread. And then there was Boris . . .

But the main problem I had with all these guys was that they lived in Brooklyn and I lived in Manhattan. These places were geographically and culturally far enough apart even under the best of circumstances, but when some mysterious person in Manhattan was trying to kill you, Brooklyn might just as well be Oz.

This was one of my problems.

Another problem was where we were driving and why. Rambam had shown me the contents of the brown envelope earlier, in the loft. It had contained a federal-government product chart, and the portion Rambam had copied listed all the poisonous chemicals and insecticides imported into America within the past year. He was rather vague about how he'd happened to come by the chart. A guy he knew in customs, he said. But the significant thing about the chart was that the chemical we were looking for, phe-noxylcholine, the one that iced our Aryan acquaintances in Bayonne, was handled by only one company in the States. The company was called Interchem, and it was located in Newark, New Jersey.

"Newark is Bayonne's uglier older sister," said Rambam, as we passed through the same depressing scenery by day that, a week before, we'd only glimpsed in the darkness.

"I'm looking forward to meeting her," I said. All around us was a landscape of industrial blight. Funnels coughing forth smoke that was a lot more dangerous than the smoke people were always bitching about that flowed cumulusly from my cigar. I didn't see anybody bitching at the funnels. Everywhere there were flat, ugly oil and gas depots and storage tanks. Occasionally, a stunted, distorted little tree that you could be pretty damn sure Joyce Kilmer had never seen.

"Actually," said Rambam, "the sunrises and sunsets in this area are supposed to be quite beautiful because of the chemicals."

"Yeah," I said, "but it looks pretty goddamn weak at high noon."

"Don't worry. We find what we're looking for, we won't be coming back."

"Alcoa can't wait."

As we neared the outskirts of Newark, where Interchem was apparently located, Rambam gestured toward the back of the Jag. "Put on that trench coat back there. With that hat over your face and the sunglasses, you ought to be fine."

"Maybe you've been watching *The Ipcress File* too much."

"Look, your face looks like a week-old Chicago-style pizza. You got to go with the hat and sunglasses, and the only thing that'll go with them is the trench coat."

"There's a logic to that."

"I'll go with the suit and tie I've got on, and let me do the talking."

"That's fine," I said, as I struggled into the trench coat. "Now that we've got our outfits worked out, who're we supposed to be?"

"We're from the EPA," said Rambam with a wicked little smile. "We're Compliance Verification agents."

"Nice touch," I said.

The two Compliance Verification agents from the EPA walked confidently through the massive warehouse piled to the ceiling with fifty-gallon drums with strange markings on them.

"Haven't seen so many drums and symbols since high-school band practice," I said.

"Beat on one of these babies, you may get a surprise," said Rambam.

Interchem, if you believed the signs, was dangerous, caustic, and corrosive. Interchem, I reflected, was, in many ways, a lot like life. Of course, if you wanted to be a philosophical nerd, everything was a lot like life. This beautiful sunset brought to you by Interchem.

We rounded a corner and headed down a drum-lined corridor toward a large, glassed-in office. I took out the walkie-talkie Rambam had given me and said a few imaginary words into it. A walkie-talkie, according to Rambam, beat a phony ID any day.

"Don't overdo it," he whispered. "Just look at some drums, write some shit in a notebook, that kind of thing. You wander around. I'll go into the office."

He went into the office.

There was a guy standing inside with a white shirt and a tie and his sleeves rolled up. I doubted if he was Mr. Interchem, but he looked like some kind of executive. Maybe a son or son-in-law. Maybe someday all this would be his.

I could see Rambam showing him some sort of ID and the two of them walking over past a desk and out of my line of vision. I started to wander around. I hoped this wouldn't take too long.

I looked at some drums. I took out a notebook and jotted down some numbers in it. Put the notebook away. Looked at some more drums. The act was getting old fast.

A few workmen in orange overalls were giving me the fish eye, so I took out the walkie-talkie, murmured a few incantations into it, looked up, and they were smoke. Amazing.

I wondered if the technique might possibly have applications in everyday life. Maybe I'd try it on an unwanted housepest some time.

A guy in a forklift was coming toward me, eyeing me suspiciously. I took out the walkie-talkie, and he hooked a left down a side corridor.

I stared at a drum and wondered if life was but a dream. Probably not, I figured. It was probably a drum.

Finally, the door to the office opened again, and Rambam came out. I put the walkie-talkie away, and we both walked briskly and importantly down the corridor, through the large warehouse, and out of the building.

He didn't talk until we were back on the turnpike.

"Wilhelm Stengal," he said. "That's our man. The only guy to order any of this stuff on Interchem's records. Only a small sample, but enough to do the job. Lives on East

Eighty-sixth Street. Yorkville. Used to be called German Town. My dad told me during the thirties the German-American *Bund* used to march there. Thousands of them filled the streets marching in full Nazi uniform."

Neither of us said anything until the desolate scenery fell away behind us and we'd reentered the Holland Tunnel. The dim, claustrophobic, unworldly eternal twilight seemed to be closing in on us.

"Apparently," I said, "a few of them are still goose-stepping around."

"I'm not *saying* she set me up, Ratso," I said. "I'm just saying that *somebody* did." Ratso was sitting on my couch wearing a labial-pink sport jacket and eating a pork pie from Myers of Keswick on Hudson Street that he'd found in my refrigerator. It was late Tuesday afternoon, and the left side of my face was beginning to clash with Ratso's sport jacket.

"You can take one look at you and see that," said Ratso with some intensity. "Somebody probably tailed your ass over to my apartment from here, then arranged to nail you on the way back."

"The streets were pretty deserted."

"So's the space between your ears," he said rather petulantly. Ratso dipped the pork pie into some residual Chinese sweet-and-sour sauce he'd also located in the refrigerator. It'd been in there for weeks, but they say it keeps.

"Pete Myers wouldn't like to see you doing that to his pork pies," I said.

"Let it be our little secret."

I walked somewhat desultorily over to the kitchen counter, poured a medicinal shot of Jameson into the old bull horn, walked over to the window, toasted another Tuesday in my tragic little life, and killed the shot. I wasn't really feeling sorry for myself; I was just confused. And I felt, down deep somewhere in my bruised bones, that something extremely ugly was about to occur.

I was all for calling in Sergeant Cooperman and picking up Wilhelm Stengal. Old traffic tickets or something. I had come to firmly believe that he was a major piece in the John Morgan puzzle. My theory was that he'd employed the two Aryans, then spliced them in Bayonne for botching the hotel job. A hard man to work for, I thought.

I also believed he was the man who'd lost the hornbill feather among the cobwebs on the floor of the croaked lawyer's office. So he'd been to Borneo. I wondered if he also wore a blue cornflower in his lapel.

Rambam had gotten Boris and a group of Brooklyn myrmidons to stake out Stengal's house on East Eighty-sixth Street. He didn't think we had enough on Stengal yet to bring Cooperman in. He felt that the Aryans had been amateurs, and that Stengal was an old-time pro. He'd also pointed out, rather gauchely I thought, that I was an amateur.

I'd seen Rambam play this cat-and-mouse game before, and I had to admit that he usually got the cat or the mouse or whoever the hell it was he was after. But in the back of my mind there was the nagging notion that he was never going to bring Cooperman into it. Rambam wanted Stengal for himself.

Rambam, I felt, wanted to hunt Nazis in New York, and I wanted to find John Morgan. What the hell, I thought, maybe we'd both get our chance.

I walked back across the loft to where Ratso was sitting and to where the pork pie was no longer in evidence. Ratso looked up at me almost belligerently. He fairly shouted:

"Maybe Carmen tied and gagged herself and hung herself by the wrists from the clothes rod at the Pierre. Maybe she killed John Morgan, switched the bodies, went back to Argentina, then came up to New York and got you involved in such a baffling, unsolvable case because she heard you were a misogynist."

"Pull your lips together for a minute, Ratso. All I'm saying is that Carmen tells a strange story, is a beautiful woman, and could be dangerous." I walked back over to the bottle of Jameson and poured a fair-sized jolt into the bull's horn.

"You *are* a misogynist!" Ratso shouted tauntingly.

I walked rather stoically over to the Sherlock Holmes head, withdrew a cigar, bit off the end, and spit it on the floor. I walked back to the kitchen window, struck a wooden match against the fashionable exposed-brick wall, and lit the cigar. A little theater never hurts when someone is attacking you for being a misogynist.

I puffed on the cigar and watched the gray clouds rolling into the Village for a few moments as if I were struggling to get control of myself. For some reason I thought of Winnie Katz. If I was a misogynist, I wondered, what the hell was she? Finally, I turned to face my accuser.

"I don't hate anyone," I said. "Maybe Wilhelm Stengal. Or what I think he represents. But I don't hate lawyers, or Negroes, or vegetarians, or homosexuals, or lesbians, or nonsmokers, or guys who go around wearing dead men's clothing and spouting newly discovered sensibilities. . . ."

Here, I killed the shot and looked Ratso in the eyes.

". . . I don't hate myself—did I mention myself?—and I don't hate cats and I don't hate dogs and I don't hate rats and I don't hate Wade Boggs and I don't hate insane people in mental hospitals who go around rhyming things to some pinhead psychiatrist so he can afford a new BMW. . . .

"I have loved certain women in my life . . . I don't

profess to love them as an ethnic group. The kind of guy that loves all women and is always pointing out tits and ass to everybody is usually a latent homosexual . . . too bad they don't have a dance class for that kind of guy. . . ."

I was standing in the living room and gesturing dramatically toward the ceiling with my cigar, and Ratso was sitting on the couch with his mouth open. In the labial-pink sport jacket and with his mouth agape, he looked like a large, disbelieving codfish.

"I don't *hate* all broads, Ratso. I just think women are wired differently. If you *love* all broads, then I feel sorry for you, because one day, my dear Ratso, fate will pluck you up by your wrinkled little scrotum and you will realize much to your chagrin that you are a latent homosexual, which, of course, is a lot less exciting than being a killer fag, but you take what you can get.

"Our heroic friendship, of course, will continue unchanged. If I should appear to be a little guarded or uneasy around you at times, I'll only be protecting my person from what others might say. We're very into images these days—in fact, we always have been. As Geronimo said, in turning down the offer of a Cadillac from the U.S. Government, 'Man ride in car—nobody looks. Man ride horse—*everybody* looks.' "

Ratso looked at me like he was ready to run me down to Dr. Bock's office again. I was ready to gut an infuriating, oversized, rather smug codfish.

Both of us were saved by a bloodcurdling scream from the street.

41

It was one of those moments many people wait a lifetime for. Some, possibly longer. I'd thrown the puppet head out the window to the dark, strange-looking figure standing next to a garbage truck in the gathering twilight. A minute or two passed before we heard the heavy footsteps in the hallway. Then three knocks resounded sharply against the door of the loft.

The housepest in the labial-pink sport jacket with whom I'd been arguing the innocence of women in general and of Carmen in particular now stood by my desk watching the door, his curiosity piqued. In a way, mine was, too.

"Come in!" I shouted.

The door opened slowly, and a figure wearing a blue backpack and carrying a smiling puppet head in one hand slithered over the threshold. He looked, for all the world, like Yessir You're-a-fart's hipper younger brother in Western drag. He walked over to me, gave me a hug, handed me the puppet head, and dumped the blue backpack squarely in the middle of the desk, where the cat sniffed at it curiously for a moment, then went back to sleep.

In silence, I walked with the puppet head over to the refrigerator, placed it securely back on its perch, returned to the desk, extracted a fresh cigar from Sherlock Holmes's head, went through the prenuptial arrangements, and fired it up.

I sat down in the chair, took a few puffs, and watched the hazy blue smoke drift lazily up to the lesbian level.

"Ratso," I said, "I'd like you to meet Ratso."

* * *

We could hear Winnie and her girls working out some-where in the near-distant homosexual heavens, but the loft itself was unusually quiet. A lot had gone down, as it were, on several different levels. On one level, for some strange reason, I hoped there was only dancing going on. But this level, for me, was one of imagination, and imagination, though worshiped by Einstein, was never trusted by Sherlock, and hadn't done me a hell of a lot of good, either.

On a more basic level, the one on which the three of us were standing, the Ratso who bore the closest resemblance to Ralph Nader now had the floor.

In 1969, according to Washington Ratso, né Jimmie Silman, a paraplegic in North Carolina named Sid White gave him the name "Ratso" after a car accident and a long convalescence had reduced him to 119 pounds and caused him to walk with a slight limp. The detailed nature of Washington Ratso's account pretty effectively defrayed any major challenges from New York Ratso. The cat and I, trusting spirits to the bitter end, took him at his word.

In 1978, again according to Washington Ratso, he was introduced to me at the Cellar Door in Georgetown by our mutual friend Tex Rubinowitz. (I don't remember the circumstances of my meeting either Ratso, but as Ingrid Bergman once said, "The recipe for happiness is good health and a bad memory." At least I think it was Ingrid Bergman.)

Apparently, I'd just fired a guitar player for "playing too good," and had hired Ratso, thereby kicking him upstairs from bass player to guitar player. "Who's gonna play bass?" he'd wanted to know. "We don't need a bass," I'd reportedly told him.

This little exchange will not be very meaningful or, I daresay, humorous to nonmusical types, but it was fun for me to hear it again since I didn't remember any of it the first time. New York Ratso was not amused.

He sat quietly as Washington Ratso went through a

hilarious recounting of our exploits later that night at Mr.
Henry's, a gay bar in Georgetown. When he got to the part
about me making eyes at the piano player, a look of confirmed suspicion came into New York Ratso's eyes, and a
slight moue of distaste crossed his face like a hint of a
shadow falling on a sunny salami sandwich. He walked to
the refrigerator in disgust, opened the door, found he'd
eaten everything already, and slammed the door so hard it
rattled the puppet head.

I poured a round for the two Ratsos and myself, and
when things settled down a bit, New York Ratso began
grudgingly to give us his story.

He'd met me in 1973 at Max's Kansas City, where he'd
heckled me from the audience with such virtuosity that my
brother, Roger, who was then managing my band, invited
him backstage. I, of course, had forgotten the incident, but
Ratso remembered everything with great clarity. It was,
for Ratso, like the day Kennedy died is to everybody else.
For me, it was another show in my hip pocket.

In 1974 Ratso met Bob Dylan. Jesus and Hitler he'd met
much earlier, he contended, while experimenting with
psychedelic drugs in Madison, Wisconsin. But it wasn't
until 1975, in a parking lot in Vermont during Bob Dylan's
Rolling Thunder Revue that Joan Baez gave Larry Sloman
the sobriquet "Ratso." She named him that, so she said at
the time, because of his unkempt and unpleasant appearance.

"Hard to believe," I said.

New York Ratso went on to point out that, though
Washington Ratso may have been a Ratso longer, he him-
self had known the Kinkster much longer. Washington
Ratso absorbed this rather stoically, and poured himself a
long one and avowed he had to get on the road pretty soon.
He suggested I look inside the blue backpack on my desk.
This was fine with me, because the dueling Ratsos were
starting to get up my sleeve.

With one Ratso looking over each shoulder, I zipped

open the backpack and extracted a large envelope from which I withdrew a black-and-white photograph. I looked at the photo, nodded my head, and congratulated Washington Ratso on being a fine stringer. He hugged me again, exchanged a chilly handshake with his New York counterpart, patted the cat, and headed back to our nation's capital.

When he'd gone, I studied the photograph again. I'd only seen the man once in my life, and that wasn't under the best of circumstances. It was in a pine box in a funeral home in Cleveland, Ohio.

Ratso, I noticed, was gazing at the photo too. "I thought I was the only Ratso in your life," he said, a trifle wistfully.

"Part of growing up," I said.

Soon Ratso too was smoke, and the cat and I were recuperating from our two housepests. I'd just taken my brontosaurus-foreskin cowboy boots off and was settling down to a quiet evening when the phones rang.

It was Rambam. His tone was urgent, and his voice was full of grim determination.

"Get ready," he said. "We're hitting Wilhelm Stengal tonight."

I had kind of had it in mind to stay in for the evening. Maybe pop some popcorn. Play Scrabble with the cat. Possibly even give Winnie Katz a call. Class didn't sound like it was in session.

I briefly ran a few of these ideas by Rambam, but they didn't fly. I told him Tuesday night was my bowling night. He was not amused.

"Look, Rambam, I'm not being a woosie here. I just don't think the idea of popping into the home of a big international Nazi who plays with poisons and kills people for kicks is exactly best foot forward." The cat nodded her head in agreement.

"Listen, Mr. Stay-at-home-baby," said Rambam almost insultingly, "we can't just sit around and solve this one by deductive reasoning. Boris and the boys have been watching this guy. Boris says the place looks like the American Embassy right before the fall of Saigon. There's barbed wire everywhere, and right now, while we're on the phone discussing this, he's out back burning papers in a barrel. We gotta move on this guy soon, or he's gonna fly south like those fucking hummingbirds you're always talking about."

There was a crude logic to what Rambam was saying. If Stengal flew the coop, a major piece of the John Morgan puzzle might be irretrievably lost. On the other hand, I had a feeling in my lower bowel that Stengal, though a mystery man himself, was not in a vastly different position than I was. Both of us, I felt, were searching for John Morgan. For John's sake, I dearly hoped I got there first.

If Stengal was indeed the blue-cornflower man, the Zyklon-B-derivative specialist, the slow-leak son-of-a-bitch who sicced the skinheads on me, he could well be an old-time Nazi. The McCoy. The real thing. As such, my attitudes toward his life or death on this planet were probably a little to the left of Zev's. The problem was, I needed Stengal. The problem also was, he thought he needed me.

In this case, it was not nice to feel needed.

"Look, Rambam," I said, "we're not going tonight. I've got a strange feeling—"

"Call it a hunch," Rambam interrupted.

"Call it whatever the hell you want, but Stengal's after more than those photographs the skinheads took from me. Think of a way to get the two of us into his house. I want to see the place. I also want him alive."

"Ah. Ve have vays to make him talk."

"That's the spirit."

"How's tomorrow sound?" Rambam asked, like he was inquiring about a racquetball game.

I told Rambam I'd think about tomorrow, and again reminded him to come up with a way to get us inside without resorting to catapulting the castle. I hung up.

The cat was asleep, but I was starting to feel kind of restless. I'd just thought about putting on my boots and drifting over to the Monkey's Paw, or the Ear, or the Lone Star when the phones rang again.

This time it was Carmen. I asked her where Ratso was, and she said she didn't know and she didn't care. She wanted to come over to my place. She thought it was time the two of us got to know each other. She sounded like she meant it in the Old Testament sense. With only a slight pang of guilt I gave her the directions to the loft. She asked if there was anything I needed. I said I'd let her know when she got here. She said she'd be over soon. I said fine. She hung up. I hung up.

I put on my brontosaurus foreskins.

If you think you may be going for a ride, it's a good thing to put on your boots.

An old friend of mine from Texas, Dr. Jim Bone, once told me an Indian legend about the content of the Milky Way. The Indians believe that the Milky Way is the lingering smoke from the distant campfires of their ancestors and friends who have gone before them and are waiting for them to arrive. Scientists, of course, know that the Milky Way is comprised of stars, subatomic particles, asteroids, inert gases, and galactic dust. That's a problem we have today: too many scientists, not enough Indians.

Be that as it may, there are some people, whom you may have met in other circumstances and whom you suddenly see sitting across the kitchen table from you and realize they could fill an emptiness in your life. Everyone has this emptiness, but some of us have it more than others. It's called being spiritually horny.

As I looked into Carmen's eyes that evening, I saw a timelessness, a warm, primitive presence capable of filling a vast emptiness, like smoke from a comforting campfire that almost lingers long enough to mend a broken heart.

I poured a couple get-acquainted shots from a bottle of Wild Turkey I found in the back of a cabinet. She was, I knew, Ratso's girlfriend, not to mention Morgan's fiancée. Over the years I'd developed a hard-hewn code of ethics; not only did I live by it, but I felt that without it, life itself would have very little meaning for me. On the other hand, I wasn't running for the school board.

We made a silent toast, killed the shots, and looked at each other with a sudden intimacy that suggested no kitchen table would ever be likely to keep us apart.

With a slightly trembling hand I poured another round, deliberately not looking into Carmen's black, unfocused, prehistoric eyes. She seemed too young to be so old. Too shy to be so bold. She grabbed my wrist and held on with her blood-red nails. I felt briefly like I was in danger of being carried off by one of those large, extinct birds with the long names. Maybe it wouldn't be so bad. With my free hand I killed the shot.

"You've got to find him," she hissed. Her voice sounded a little like air escaping from the tire of a lox-colored '58 Cadillac tearing ass south down the Pan-American Highway in the middle of August. I was at the wheel, and I knew

I was in some danger of losing control of my motor vehicle.

"Him?" I said. It was an interesting pronoun, I thought. But then, we lived in a world of interesting pronouns. Fairly tedious people sometimes, but interesting pronouns.

"John," she said.

"I see."

I didn't, of course. All I saw for sure was Carmen letting go of my wrist, downing her shot of Wild Turkey, squirming seductively in her chair, and unbuttoning two buttons on the top of her blouse. She was definitely headlighting with her brights on.

The Turkey was opening her up in more ways than one, apparently. She began talking rather freely. As they say in the argot of the West, I let her have her head.

". . . never had a strong, masculine figure to look up to . . . I can still recall my parents arguing when I was a child. My dad would come home late. I was already in bed, but I could hear my mother saying, 'Stay away from me, Bill. Don't come near me when you smell that way. . . .'"

I murmured something about alcoholism not being unknown in Latin cultures. Then I poured us both another round, sat back, and waited for more from Carmen.

". . . so I grew up always wanting a strong, take-charge kind of man. A man who cracks a subtle whip . . . who'll tell me what to do . . . who'll never let me fall . . ."

I sat up a little straighter in my chair. I was thinking of what Charles Manson had said to Squeaky Fromme when they'd first met. They were walking down the street somewhere—I think it was San Francisco—and Squeaky slipped, but Charlie caught her before she hit the ground. He held her tightly by the arm and said, "I'll never let you fall."

That macho, take-charge, ride-'em-hard-and-put-'em-away-wet routine works with more broads in this liberated age than the *Ms.* magazine editorial board would care to admit. Or maybe it's just that the Squeaky Fromme gets the grease. Whatever it was, I found myself standing so close to Carmen I could feel her nipples boring into my chest. They were harder than Japanese arithmetic.

I felt a sexy, half-human, half-reptilian kind of claw encircle and slowly close around my *pisang*. It was, in all honesty, a not-unpleasant sensation. *Pisang* is the Malay word for "banana."

I closed my eyes.

The next thing I saw was the unwelcome visage of Ratso's large and loyal face looming up suddenly before me like an image shot from a magic lantern. Then I saw Morgan smiling cheerfully at me across time and geography. I pushed Carmen away.

I walked to the table on fairly unsteady wheels, killed my shot of Turkey, and turned to Carmen. Her arms were groping blindly toward me. Her upper lip was perspiring. She looked like a cranked-up, slightly over-the-hill Menudo groupie. A kinder, more classically oriented eye might've regarded her as a Thisbe, in a randy moment, reaching impossibly through the garden wall for her Pyramus.

"Maybe," I said weakly, "maybe if Ratso'd never met you, if John Morgan hadn't loved you, if you and I had met somewhere else, maybe in the Peace Corps . . . I could've found it possible for us to have made love. Even now, with—"

Carmen had stormed to the door of the loft. She flung it open wide enough for any eavesdropping lesbian to hear. "I don't *make love*," she shouted, "I *fuck!*"

Then the door slammed. Then the cat and I stared in silence at the closed door. Then we listened to the not-quite-mechanical whine of the freight elevator descending downward into the worldly world.

Then I killed Carmen's shot.

44

To take my mind off of Carmen, I called an old friend of mine, John Rapp. John was the *shabbos goy* of the Blue Nun Wine Company and somewhat of an expert in your Teutonic area. At least I once saw one of those old World War I kraut skypieces with the pointy-looking spike on top at his apartment. Rapp was also the proud possessor of a Luftwaffe toilet-paper holder stamped with the date 1944, an eagle, and a swastika. Rapp had been a country-music lover, and a fan of mine in particular, dating back to about the time the Kaiser first waxed his cookie-duster. I had a certain loyalty to my fans. Even if they eventually turned out to be hatchet-murderers, I somehow tended to trust their judgment. Besides, I thought it might be a good idea to know a little about Wilhelm Stengel's fortress in the event that Rambam and I ever got on the same wavelength long enough to assault it.

"I'm a *Judenfreund* from way back," said Rapp when I got him on the line.

"Good," I said. "Maybe you'll be more help this time around." I briefly sketched the situation for John and gave him the address of Stengal's brownstone. He knew the place.

Apparently, it had had a long and sinister history, going back to its first owner, who was the *Bund* leader at the time. Though most of the old places in Yorkville had now been transformed into condos and trendy Japanese restaurants, this address had curiously—or possibly not so curiously—

remained in the same fascist hands. Rapp suspected there were quite a lot of relics inside the place but, as a *Judenfreund,* recommended I stay the hell away from it. I asked him for an assessment of what the mentality of the current owner might be.

Rapp said, "Like the guy who kept pigeons in *The Producers.* Remember, Kinkster?"

I told him I remembered, thanked him, and hung up. And I did remember. More than I wanted to about the Germans. I was too young to have been there at the time, but I was a Jew. There would always be a little piece of yesterday in my eye.

It was around nine o'clock when I lay down for a little power nap on the couch. Every time I closed my eyes, I saw Carmen. I recognized the folly of following my *pisang* around the world, but I had wanted Carmen and, apparently, I wanted her now. Though I had been loyal to Ratso, I knew that, like Jimmy Carter, I had lusted in my heart. Of course, I reflected, if you go around worrying about lusting in your heart all the time, you'll probably never get near the front of the line for having big fun on the bayou. Even with the excess baggage that Judaism sometimes brings, I was suddenly very glad that I wasn't a Christian fundamentalist.

I closed my eyes and thought of Carmen again.

The phones rang. Could it be? I wondered, as I got up from the couch and moved quickly for the desk.

It was not Carmen.

It was a heavy Germanic voice that said, "Herr Friedman?"

"Yeah?"

"Your friend Ratso . . . I'm sorry to say that he is dead."

The caller hung up, and for a moment I sat there stunned, listening to the dial tone. Then I hung up and, with a sense of dread, picked up the blower again and dialed Ratso's number in New York. I got his answering machine. I hung up.

Frantically, I dialed Washington Ratso's number. It rang five times, and then I got *his* answering machine. I was trying to sort things out, but as I hung up the blower I noticed my hand was shaking. I felt in my guts that it had been no crank call that I had received.

They say home is where the answering machine is. I could wait awhile and call both numbers again, I thought. I could leave urgent messages at each place. But one idea kept coming into my head, and it was having a rather numbing visceral effect.

I was suddenly very much afraid that I was no longer a two-Ratso man.

They say you never marry the person you first see *Casablanca* with. They say a lot of things, I thought, as Rambam sliced a vicious right turn off Eighth Avenue onto Fourteenth Street, and they're usually right.

It was ten o'clock, and I didn't know where my children were. I wasn't even sure I had any. All I knew was we were on our way to Wilhelm Stengal's house and Rambam had a plan. I liked a man with a plan.

Before I'd left the loft, I recruited Rambam to help with the Ratso situation. By the time he'd arrived, I'd already called the numbers in New York and Washington several times, leaving urgent messages to get in touch with me at the loft. I gave Rambam the two addresses, watched him make a terse phone call, and did not feel particularly reassured when he promised me he'd be putting a few "Hebraic irregulars" on it.

To begin with, Rambam had never especially liked New York Ratso, nor did he particularly put much credence in the veracity of the kraut caller's statement. In fact, with another human being in the loft, taking nothing away from the cat, I was beginning to wonder if the call mightn't have been an effort at Bavarian humor myself. Knowing Rambam's distaste for one Ratso, I did not feel it necessary to inform him that the other Ratso was a Lebanese Druse.

Finally, in a mood that had begun to vaseline back and forth between doubt and dark desperation, I'd called Cooperman. After I'd related the situation to him, he'd made what sounded like a sort of choking noise on the phone. Before things became too unpleasant, I was able to give him the actual names and the addresses of the two Ratsos, and he was able to tell me that he would do nothing for twenty-four hours, at which time I could file a missing-persons report if I so wished. Then we were both able to hang up.

Now Rambam was taking the FDR like a hack honing in on LaGuardia. The FDR Drive ran along the East River like a narrow, pock-marked ramp to hell, and hell was as good a name as any for where we were going. Every time the Jag hit a pothole, Rambam cursed and I screwed my cowboy hat on a little tighter. It was a nightmarish ride, but it beat the subway.

"In just a minute you're gonna have to lose that cowboy hat," said Rambam, as he wrenched us off the FDR onto Ninety-sixth Street. "I've got another one for you to wear though."

"Good," I said. "That's the one thing that cowboys and Jewboys have in common. We both like to wear our hats indoors, and we attach a certain amount of importance to it."

"Well, unless we fuck up real bad, you should get a chance to wear a hat indoors tonight."

"Great," I said, as I flung the cowboy hat into the back of the Jag. "Where's the new hat?"

"It's in the trunk," Rambam said almost to himself as we cruised silently up Eighty-sixth Street.

"That's too bad."

"It sure is," said Rambam as he looked at my hair. I lowered the visor and looked in the mirror. My head looked like a rocket ship. My hair had congealed like a gelatin mold into the shape of the inside of the cowboy hat. I'd seen this before. It was an occupational hazard afflicting cowboys with kinky hair and Jewboys who, for inexplicable reasons of their own, insisted upon wearing cowboy hats. Which of the two categories I belonged to depended on how you looked at it. Most people, for reasons of esthetics, preferred not to.

"Dis looks like de place, boss," said Rambam, pointing out a stately brownstone on the left-hand side of the street. The lights were on inside, giving the building a distinguished, romantic, almost merry appearance. It looked like Nick and Nora Charles might live there. Unfortunately, they didn't.

Rambam made another pass around the block, checked the street carefully, and finally parked the Jag about a block and a half away from the place. We got out of the car, and Rambam walked over to a nearby pay phone and dialed a number. I readjusted my moss as best I could, nodded to a passing young couple, and edged closer to hear Rambam's conversation.

". . . Yes, sir . . . this is Mr. Wallenberg with Con Ed . . . we've received a field report about a potential emergency situation in your area. Our Main Number Thirty-seven on the East Side appears to have ruptured, and we're concerned about the possibility of emissions into residential dwellings. . . . Yeah, within the hour . . . an Emissions Detection Team . . . they're in the area right now . . . no problem . . ."

Rambam walked back to the Jag with a satisfied smirk on his face. "Jesus Christ," I said. "Wallenberg?"

"You can call me Raoul, or you can call me Ray," he said as he opened the trunk.

Five minutes later the Emissions Detection Team was heading up the sidewalk at a leisurely pace toward Wilhelm Stengal's house. We were wearing yellow regulation hard-hats, bright orange safety vests, and thick leather equipment belts loaded with enough gear to hot-wire the Hindenburg.

Out of the corner of my eye I saw Rambam transfer a small black handgun from his vest pocket to the small of his back. "That's the one piece of equipment," I said, "that I damn well don't want to see you use."

Rambam smiled.

"Think about it," he said. "Here we are going into the home of a World War II Nazi to warn him that he may be in danger of being gassed." Rambam laughed a faraway laugh.

"The irony," I said "is not lost on me."

"Germany," said Wilhelm Stengal, "is the only country in the world that could rise like a phoenix from the ashes of destruction." It's pretty hard to argue with an elderly fanatic. Especially one who's pointing a Luger at your nose.

I cast a nervous look at Rambam, who was standing about ten feet over to my right and looking like he was ready to wring Stengal's scrawny neck. Stengal was beginning to resemble some kind of horrific chicken, with his slightly stooped shoulders, thin, cordy neck, and large, civilized-appearing head. His hand on the Luger was steady as they come.

"The West Germans, in particular, have done well," I said, humoring the old man. "I understand they've come up with a new microwave oven. Seats forty."

This drew no response from Rambam. With Stengal, however, it was a different matter. His hand tightened almost imperceptibly on the Luger, and for a moment, in the gothic, art-museum lighting of the place, I thought I could see millions of men and military machinery moving behind his gray eyes. Then he did something that chilled me. He let forth with a laugh that sounded more like a cackle. An intelligent, arrogant, almost nostalgic cackle that bubbled with evil.

They say when you laugh, the whole world laughs with you, and they're usually right. Usually.

Just how Inspector Clouseau and I permitted ourselves to get into a situation where an old geezer was pointing a dangerous-looking war relic at my beezer is something neither of us, I'm sure, is particularly proud of. Essentially, he outfoxed us.

I'd told Rambam before we went into the place that we should work on our story, and he said we'd be out of there before we needed a story. I reflected bitterly upon this as Stengal deftly shifted the Luger from his right hand to his left one, and checked the time like the old pro that he was. There was a swastika inside a circle on the handgrip of the Luger. It really was an old war relic, and so was Stengal, and God only knew what might be going on in the ancient, dusty, twisted gray matter department of a World War II Nazi. Maybe he was still following orders.

The other mistake Rambam and I had made was to allow ourselves to be separated. If you're ever visiting an old Nazi's house under the guise of a gas company Emissions Detection Team, always stick together and let one guy do all the talking.

What had actually occurred was that Rambam had wandered off through the living room with an emissions detection device that appeared to fascinate Stengal. It was a scam, Rambam later maintained, that was extremely effective, especially with elderly people. He'd enclosed a light meter in a portentous-looking leather case with only the dial exposed, and as he walked toward the light fixture in the far corner of the room, the thing went crazy. Stengal definitely appeared to be hooked, walking nervously alongside Rambam, wringing his hands. It was at that point that I drifted into a huge adjoining room whose contents would've made the lions in front of the Metropolitan Museum of Art turn green with envy.

If you're one of these pointy-headed intellectual sticklers for the facts, you might point out, probably with your head, that the lions are in front of the library, not the museum of art. To this, however, I would answer, Under the circumstances, what possible difference could it make? Read between the lions.

Unfortunately, I know so little about art that I don't even know what I like, but, unless I missed my bet, this room represented a treasure trove of works that must've been pillaged by the SS from museums and private collections all over Europe. I confess to being mesmerized.

I was staring into the faintly familiar Flemish face of a woman who seemed to be saying, "I don't belong here. Please take me home with you, mister," when another voice sounded very close to my left ear. It was also faintly familiar.

"On which side of town is your office located?" asked Wilhelm Stengal very slowly and distinctly. I realized my answer would be a coin toss. I did not turn around.

"East Side," I said finally. When I felt the gun in my

back, I knew that Rambam must've told him "West Side."

Such a simple trap, I thought, and there was nothing I could do. East is East and West is West. Especially to a kraut.

I looked up into the friendly face of the Flemish woman. "I don't belong here either," I said.

Stengal motioned with the Luger for me to get over closer to where Rambam was standing. I did. We were back in the main room of the house. I never went in for art museums much anyway.

"You have your friend John Morgan to thank for this," Stengal said. "I cannot let you go now."

"Where is John Morgan?" I asked.

"When I find him," said Stengal rather ominously, "I'll extend to him your regrets. You're the first to try this here, but others, like John Morgan, have tried many times before in South America and other places. Their bodies are occasionally found floating in the Amazon with their testicles in their mouths."

It was not a pleasant image. I'd heard of pulling a groin, but this sounded, at the very least, unsportsmanlike.

When I looked at Stengal's face again, he was wearing a hideous, forced kind of smile, vaguely reminiscent of an air-scoop vent on a '65 Pontiac.

"I had to do what I had to do," said Stengal, more serious and strident now. "I was, after all, protecting the greatest genius the world has ever known!" I looked over to Rambam. He appeared to be biding his time. Unfortunately, it didn't seem as if there was going to be a lot of that left to bide.

"And you still are, aren't you, Stengal?" I asked.

Stengal turned his distinguished eyes toward me and looked directly at me, giving nothing away. He would've made a good poker player, for a Nazi.

Imperceptibly, he nodded. "I cannot let you go," he repeated almost sadly, like a rather stilted jilted lover. "Franz and Erik will be here shortly, and then—"

There was the sound of crashing glass in the front of the house. The three of us turned toward the noise, and less than an instant later the room seemed to be enveloped in smoke and flames. My throat suddenly constricted and became very dry. I was struggling for breath in a rolling blanket of searing heat. Flames leaped up all around us, effectively trapping the three of us in what appeared to be an almost certain dance of death. Just before I heard a motorcycle roar off into the night, I was vaguely aware of a voice that shouted "Never Again!"

It was an irony that was not lost upon me.

The next thing I remember was Rambam knocking me down with his shoulder and hollering, "Hit the floor!," which, under the circumstances, were easy directions. At the same time, Stengal, coughing, choking, and dodging flames, squeezed off two rounds with the Luger into the air space I'd very recently vacated. The second shot grazed Rambam's left side and made him angrier than an Italian-Jewish bull. He went straight for Stengal like a hate-seeking missile. I stayed on the floor beneath the heavy smoke level and crawled toward the action. It wasn't hard to follow just from the audio portion—coughing and choking sounds, two more shots, a series of retreating Germanic curses, and, several times, a loud and decidedly Brooklyn refrain: "I'll tear your fucking heart out! I'll tear your fucking heart out!"

I got to sort of a hallway where the smoke wasn't quite as bad, and caught sight of two scurrying figures racing down a spiral staircase. Stengal might've been o-l-d, but he could still m-o-v-e when the notion took him. Walking like a homo erectus again, I followed Rambam's broad back through a doorway into some kind of basement. The fire was beginning to crackle pretty good upstairs. I could hear sirens in the distance. Smoke was already starting to drift down into the basement.

"I don't believe it," said Rambam, as he leveled a few furious, futile kicks at an iron door. "The fucker's got a *bunker* down here."

At that moment steel bars on rollers began rolling down from the ceiling to the floor, effectively shutting Wilhelm Stengal away to a lonely death. "The way this building's going up," said Rambam, "he doesn't have a chance in there. He'll die just like 'the greatest genius the world has ever known.'"

"I don't think he was referring to *that* 'greatest genius,'" I said, watching the smoke start to billow into the basement. "I think he was talking about another 'greatest genius.'"

"Yeah? Well, let's hope the two of us are smart enough to get our asses out of here alive."

For a while, which seemed like a torturous eternity, it didn't seem like we would be. Running back up the basement stairs to the first floor, we were met by a virtual wall of fire. We returned to the basement and began, like two large, white, increasingly frantic rats in a maze, to look about for doors or windows that just weren't there. Things did not look too promising. One corner of the basement was set up as sort of a chemical laboratory with trays and test tubes and beakers, but of course there wasn't a hell of a lot of time to check it out.

I wasn't afraid to die. I'd died onstage a number of times

in my life. But I hadn't died yet in Wilhelm Stengal's basement.

I raced up the stairs again until I met with a wave of heat and could go no farther. On my way down again I looked up in despair and spotted something I hadn't seen before. It was about ten feet off the ground, but it looked like a small painted-over window high above the basement steps on the street side of the house. I yelled for Rambam and grabbed what looked like a ceremonial dagger off a nearby table.

Moments later, I was standing on Rambam's shoulders, smashing the window with the pommel of the dagger and shouting for help. I heard voices outside, knocked shards of glass away with the dagger, and, just as the heat and acrid smoke were becoming unbearable, two arms reached through the window and helped pull me out. The arms were attached to Detective-Sergeant Mort Cooperman.

A short while later, Rambam and I were on the sidewalk watching Wilhelm Stengel's empire burn. I showed Rambam the blade of the dagger. It read: *"Blut und Ehre."*

"That's 'Blood and Honor,' " said Rambam. "That was the motto of the SS. Stengal was an SS man."

"Nice guy like Wilhelm? Who'd have thought it?"

Fox and Cooperman walked up to us. "That's a nice outfit, Tex," said Cooperman. "Meter reading might be a swell midlife career change for you."

"That's what I thought."

"We're takin' you two in as material witnesses," said Fox. "Probably more than that before we're through with you."

They frisked us both and took Rambam's gun. Cooperman took the ceremonial dagger and studied it appreciatively.

"Looks almost like it might be stolen property, doesn't it, Fox?"

"Damned if it don't."

"It may *look* like stolen property, but it's not," I said, as they hustled the two of us into the back of a plain-wrapped car.

"It's an heirloom," I said to the back of Mort Cooperman's head as he gunned the engine and tore out of there. "It's been in the family almost twenty minutes."

It was one o'clock the next afternoon, Wednesday, by the time Wolf Nachman, the greatest lawyer in the world, was able to get Rambam back to Brooklyn and me back to my cat. I won't bore you with the shunting around from place to place, the holding cells, the bologna sandwiches, or the constant onslaught of tedium from Cooperman and Fox.

Needless to say, I did not get my ceremonial dagger back. Wolf said he'd work on it.

The cat appeared relatively happy to see me, and the blinking red light on the answering machine indicated that four Americans had tried to reach me during the night. I petted the cat and walked over to the machine. I put it on "rewind," took a cigar out of Sherlock's head, fired it up, leaned back in the chair, and set the machine on "play."

The first voice, to my great relief, was New York Ratso's. He sounded guarded, almost unfriendly. He'd been out to a hockey game and then hit a few bars. He wanted to meet me for lunch today at Big Wong's. There were a few things he thought we ought to talk over.

Now that I knew he was alive, I didn't especially want to go to Big Wong's and talk with Ratso. I didn't know what Carmen had told him but I could imagine, and I almost didn't care. And I was starting to feel tired as hell.

The second message was a rather heavy-handed hang-up. Nothing wrong with that. Some people just don't like to talk to answering machines. Some people really enjoy talking to answering machines. It's a diverse and fascinating world we live in. I took a puff on the cigar and pondered the world for about a microsecond.

The third message was from my old friend Cleve, once the manager of the Lone Star Cafe, now residing at the Pilgrim State Psychiatric Hospital. It's never a really good idea to establish too close a relationship with people in mental hospitals, because one day, usually sooner than you expect, they get out and try to cut your head off. But Cleve claimed he was now in a rehabilitation work-therapy program, and he had a great idea he couldn't wait to tell me about. I could wait.

I figured Cleve wasn't going anywhere, so I'd get back to him when I found out what the situation was with Washington Ratso, fed the cat, and got some sleep.

The last message on the tape took care of whatever lingering doubts I'd had about my little Lebanese brother. The voice was gruff and all too familiar. It was Sergeant Cooperman.

"More bad news for you, Tex . . . I don't know what you've got yourself into, but I'm sure as hell going to find out. Just after we released you to Nachman we got a call from a precinct outside of Washington, D.C. Guy they think is named Jimmie Silman was found burned beyond recognition in his car. The dental records are going to the lab, but the car was his and it was parked in the garage of Silman's house. The garage was destroyed, but they saved the house. And whose name and phone number do you think they found on a pad by his telephone?"

Almost unconsciously, I reached into a desk drawer and took out a kaffiyah, the traditional headgear worn by Arab peoples, and held it in my lap. It'd been sent to me by a Palestinian girl I'd once known.

I heard Cooperman's voice in the blower: ". . . Tex? You still with me, Tex?"

No, I thought, I wasn't.

I gazed at the Peace Corps photograph that had almost certainly, cost Jimmie Silman his life. The eyes stared back at me like a stranger in a dream. I looked over into the near distance of the kitchen window. Somewhere in the dancing motes of dust threading their way through the gray afternoon light, I saw the other John Morgan whom I knew so well. I saw the glint of green in his impish, mischievous eyes. For a moment, I saw his face smiling playfully back at me.

". . . John . . . you ol' devil . . . what in Christ's name have you gotten me into?"

I slept pretty well that night but I woke up with the kind of headache you'd get if you'd been drinking cheap champagne from a size-14 Cinderella slipper. There was cat vomit on the bed. The phones were ringing, so I stumbled over to the desk to answer them. It was, I noticed between waves of cranial pain, only nine o'clock.

"Kink," said a voice, "this is Kent Perkins in L.A. I've got something kind of interesting for you."

"I hope so," I said. Kent was an old friend of mine, also from Texas, but I'd met him some years ago out on the Left Coast. He was a big, friendly guy, a producer for NBC television, and, unlike my amateur self, a real private detec-

tive. Kent was married to Ruth Buzzi, the actress and come-
dienne who'd first made her mark on *Laugh-In* hitting people over the head with her purse. At the moment, in fact,
it seemed like Ruth was hitting me over the head with her
purse.

"A guy died a few days ago," Kent said, "in an old folks'
home out in the Valley. When they started trying to contact the relatives on file about the disposition of his few
effects, they all turned out to be nonexistent. He was a
Canadian citizen, apparently, but of European ancestry.
Anyway, I start going through this guy's stuff, and I get the
definite feeling he's deliberately concealing his past. In
fact, I begin to think . . ."

Kent droned on along with my head for a few moments.
The cat made a rather clumsy jump onto the desk, wobbled
silently, and sat down looking kind of embarrassed. My
head was really pounding.

". . . so I figured the guy must be some high-ranking
Nazi."

My ears perked up at the word.

"Nazi?" I said weakly.

"Not only that, but I checked over his phone bills, and
two weeks ago he made a call to a number I recognized. It
was rather unusual, I thought, for him to be calling this
particular phone number. The number, my friend, is
yours."

After I'd rung off with Kent I had a lot to think about,
but I didn't really feel like thinking. I started to make some
espresso, but then I decided not to. I fed the cat some tuna,
but she didn't want any. She was definitely off her feed.

The cat looked at me with slightly crossed eyes like
Siamese cats do. Only she wasn't Siamese. She was a New
York alley cat that I'd found in Chinatown, so she must be
Chinese. And I liked to think she had enough Jewish up-
bringing that, if a cat Hitler ever came along, she could be

in real trouble. But I knew there wasn't much danger of that ever happening. Cats are a very independent and free-dom-loving race of people.

I was feeling a bit dizzy, so I went to the couch to lie down for a little power nap. I knew the cat was ill, but just at the moment I didn't much feel like putting her in a pillowcase, lugging her down to the vet in the Village, and standing around in the waiting room with a large number of adult men and their little toy chihuahuas.

The pounding in my brain seemed to be easing up just a hair, and vague, blurry images began appearing in a light red backdrop on the inside of my eyelids. I saw a twisted old Left Coast Nazi sitting, in full uniform, under a large umbrella on a redwood verandah gazing out over Malibu and then dialing my number. I saw Wilhelm Stengal walking elegantly through the lobby of the Pierre Hotel with a blue cornflower in his lapel and with eyes that could change so suddenly from cultured mother-of-pearl to those of an angry skink whose rock's just been turned over and who can't decide whether to run for his life or to swallow the sun. Does a skink have eyes? I'd have to look it up when I got home. Then I saw Jimmie Silman's sad dark eyes. I wanted to help him, but I couldn't. I wanted to warn him, but it was too late.

The last thing I remember before I passed out was turning my head and watching the cat gamely trying to jump onto her rocking chair. Once, twice, three times she tried. Each time she fell unceremoniously back to the floor. It was painful for me to see. But if you're a cat and someone is watching you, it's worse than death.

Of course, neither the cat nor I realized at the time how close to death it actually was.

50

"Open the windows! Jesus Christ! Don't light a match! Call the Con Ed emergency number!"

Very fuzzily, I heard one strident female voice giving orders, and another, softer one, murmuring assent. Suddenly, it had become very cold, and I found myself shivering. I opened my eyes and saw a woman's face bending over me.

"Ruth Buzzi?" I asked.

"No," said Winnie Katz, "but I'd like to meet her."

She put a warm hand on my forehead. "Why did you do it?" she asked.

When you've done a lot of things in your life, this is always a confusing question. What was she talking about? Could she have found out about Rambam bugging the shrink's office?

"You've got so much to live for! If we hadn't come around and gotten in through the window by the fire escape, you'd be dead. The room's filled with gas!"

It was news to me. Of course, it accounted for everything rather neatly. I hadn't smelled anything in seven years, but this was the first time my beezer'd almost let me down for the count. How could it have happened? My mind was whirring with questions, theories, paranoid notions. My teeth were chattering. Winnie was looking down at me with deep platonic sympathy.

"Where's the cat?" I shouted.

Winnie and the other girl began looking around the place and calling for the cat the way people do who don't know much about cats. I sat up on the couch and shivered.

"Find him a coat," Winnie ordered the other girl.

"Find the cat!" I shouted. I was still too weak to stand. "Check under that rocking chair."

Winnie checked under the rocking chair and extracted a very foggy cat. One would think, after a near-death situation such as this, that a man and a cat would be experiencing a joyous reunion. One can picture the man and the cat running toward each other across the bridge of life. This, however, was not to be. The cat sat up very erect, with her back to me and her eyes on the far wall, doing a slow burn. Under other circumstances, I might've thought this behavior somewhat humorous. Things being as they were, I found it totally uncalled for.

Winnie sent the other broad upstairs, led me to the kitchen table, got the espresso machine humming a familiar aria, and got me into a heavy black lamb's wool coat that made me look like a slightly anemic pimp. Uptown Judy had given me the coat, and it was a hell of an item. A boyfriend of hers who'd been running from the law left it in her apartment and never came back. She had a very private garage sale one night, and I got the coat. If I could stay alive long enough, I thought, I ought to give her a call. Let her know how the coat was doing. Then there was Downtown Judy. But my mind was wandering. I looked up and saw Winnie expertly pouring the espresso.

"You're going to make somebody a very fine something someday," I said.

"You silver-tongued shithead," she said as she handed me the cup.

I took a sip and looked at Winnie. She was a very pretty girl. She had freckles. She had intelligent, sexy, hazel eyes. She had a very comforting presence about her.

"You saved my life," I said.

"That's what they all say," she said.

* * *

By the time the two Con Ed guys got there, I was striding back and forth in my Uptown Judy pimp coat with an unlit cigar in my mouth lecturing Winnie about how sometimes a cigar is just a cigar. She'd made a comment I hadn't liked, and I felt called upon to defend my oral dissertation. The Con Ed guys pretty much ignored the two of us and went to work in the vicinity of the oven. I did notice they did not have an emissions detection device.

The effect of the gas had fairly well worn off by now, except that I had a bit of a buzz going for myself. Winnie was listening to me with rather a smart-ass schoolgirl smile that was kind of fetching in an offbeat way.

". . . Freud said that every human being has the potential to be homosexual. It's an accident that we become heterosexual, determined by developmental vicissitudes. So you see, cigar smoking is really no big deal. Dr. Charles Ansell, the head shrink of the San Fernando Valley and a personal friend of our family, maintains that it 'suggests an unresolved infantilism reminiscent of suckling of the breast.' Dr. Ansell maintains that it can also, of course, suggest fellatio, but you can't have everything. Care for a cigar?"

"Hey, buddy," one of the Con Ed guys said, motioning me over to the stove, "you want to see what the trouble was?"

"Yeah," I said. I walked over next to him. He pointed to an area close to the floor and behind the oven.

"Flex hose worked its way loose," he said.

"How often does this kind of thing happen?" I asked.

"Depends," said the Con Ed guy, "on whether there's an inch-and-a-quarter wrench available."

51

In Austin, when you die, they say you go to Willie Nelson's house. As I sat at my desk that evening listening to an old Billy Joe Shaver record on the Victrola, I reflected upon a time some years back when I'd gone to Willie Nelson's house without having to make the ultimate sacrifice. Willie'd told me something that night that made quite an impression on my pillow for many years to come. He'd said, "If you ain't crazy, there's something wrong with you."

As I listened to the garbage trucks growling along with Billy Joe, I poured a second shot of Wild Turkey into the old bull's horn, flicked a Clarence Darrow–length cigar ash into my Texas-shaped ashtray, and realized that there was nothing wrong with me.

So I had to be crazy.

That would explain a lot of things.

It would explain why, two weeks after returning from Cleveland, I was still on a wild-goose chase looking for John Morgan. It would explain why a lot of people—namely Zev, Rambam, and Winnie Katz—seemed to be saving my life lately. It would explain why I was ready to believe that a World War II Nazi, now residing, thankfully, in whatever the kraut version of Willie Nelson's house is, had called me from southern California as Kent Perkins maintained, and invited me, as I was now beginning to realize, to John Morgan's funeral. They wanted to be certain I didn't get on the trail of the *other* John Morgan. They probably hadn't known it would be an open casket funeral!

Maybe I'd call Cleve and have him reserve a bed for me

at Pilgrim State, I thought as I killed the shot of Turkey. It was heavier than Jameson. It was sweeter than Jack Daniel's. It was still pretty damn good if you didn't have the other two. I poured another shot.

So I was crazy. I was a little out of line with the other ducks. Out where the buses don't run. The date on my carton, apparently, had expired. There was nothing wrong with me. I was crazy.

How else could I justify my conviction that some Nazi conspiracy of international proportions was after my ass? Was there a functioning, death-dealing 88 organization? Was this a brotherhood of evil feasting at some satanic banquet, or was I nodding out at a local Lion's Club luncheon?

But with Wilhelm Stengal now a crispy critter, how else could I explain the vengeful irony of method in the morning's attack upon my life and the life of my cat? And with Wilhelm Stengel now a member of the grateful dead —not the rock group—could anyone have known about the gas-leak business Rambam and I had visited upon him?

I thought briefly of going down for another check-up-from-the-neck-up with Dr. Bock, but I didn't want to give Ratso, Rambam, and McGovern the satisfaction. Beyond a doubt, the whole world was crazy and I was a part of that world, and when I thought about it, I wouldn't have wanted it any other way. I killed the last shot and went to bed.

52

Friday morning Jimmie Silman, aka Washington Ratso, called. I didn't know if I was in Willie Nelson's house or still dreaming. Fortunately, neither was the case.

"Ratso," I said. "Jesus Christ, man, where are you? Goddamn, brother, what happened?"

"Well, let's take the first epithet first. I'm standing in what's left of my house. The place is gutted, my guitars are slightly damp, the car is gone, and the garage is gone. I've been talking to the neighbors and the police, and now I understand that *I* was almost gone. I wander off with a broad for twenty-four hours and *this* shit happens."

"That's the vengeance of Muhammad being visited upon you for practicing fornication."

"I was raised as a *Methodist*, for Christ's sake, and I stopped practicing fornication when I was about twelve years old. By now I'm pretty good at it. At least that's what the broad told me. You ever seen a water-logged 1957 Stratocaster guitar built by Tex Rubinowitz?"

"I'm afraid not. Ratso, I don't want to bring up anything unpleasant, but who was in the car?"

"Yeah, that was pretty unpleasant, all right. The cops think it was the guy from AAA. For twenty-four hours after I called them they kept threatening to send someone over to start the car and they never did, so I just left a note on the garage door. Apparently, when I was out with the broad, he finally made it over. He started it up, and the bomb blew him away. Christ."

Before I hung up, I told Ratso what had happened to me

the previous morning, warned him to be extremely careful, and let him know how great it felt for me to be a two-Ratso man again. I was thrilled he was alive and well and I wanted to share the experience, as they say in Hollywood, with someone. I thought about calling New York Ratso, but I couldn't be sure he wouldn't tell Carmen, and I was less sure than ever about Carmen. Also, I didn't want to create feelings of ambivalence in Ratso, letting him know he was the only Ratso in my life for a brief, shining moment but that now the other Ratso had come back into the picture.

I tried to call McGovern, but he was away from his desk. I was away from my desk too. Pouring a shot of Wild Turkey into a cup of espresso and feeding the cat her morning tuna.

Finally, I settled on calling Rambam. I laid out the whole Washington Ratso situation for him, told him my great relief that Jimmie Silman was alive, and told him who the cops now suspected the actual victim was.

"I'm glad it wasn't Ratso," I said, "but it's a shame about the AAA guy."

"That's nothing," said Rambam. "I know a Mafia don who lives right here in Brooklyn. Every morning he calls AAA to start his car."

"Gas leaks are more common than you think," said New York Ratso as we sat at a little table in Big Wong's that afternoon. "I had one in my apartment last year. Same thing happened. Guys came out and wanted to know if it'd been tampered with. Hell, I told 'em, that stove's never even been used. They don't want you to know how often it happens." He lifted a rather large portion of roast pork scrambled eggs into his mouth with a Chinese soup spoon.

I was beginning to have my doubts too. Wilhelm Stengal was at Willie Nelson's house, John Morgan might be there too, for all I knew, and I hadn't been beaten up since the last time I'd been with Ratso. Quite possibly, the whole case had died with Stengal. The other theory, that we were dealing with a huge, nefarious, Hitlerian Hydra, lopping one of its skinheads off only to produce ten more, was looking less and less plausible in the pale light of a fading February afternoon in comforting, immutable Chinatown. March was almost here, and I, for one, was ready to goose-step into a new month and a new frame of mind. Get a little mental health on board. Time for visions and revisions.

On the other hand, there was the mysterious phone call Kent Perkins had reported. And there was one less AAA representative in the District of Columbia area. I didn't know what to think. What I need, I thought, is one single shred of hard evidence.

"What I need," said Ratso, "is some duck sauce for this roast duck–roast pork over rice."

"No doubt," I said. "Ratso, I want you to do a favor for me."

"Anything you want, except I won't share the roast pork scrambled eggs."

"I know things may be a little strained between us right now. I haven't been as open with you as maybe I could about this case."

"Why is this case different from all other cases? You never tell me shit."

"Well, I'll tell you something now. I started out looking for my friend John Morgan, and now I feel I'm surrounded by enemies and I'm not even sure who they are or even whether they exist. And I'll tell you something else, in case you may be wondering. I did not hose Carmen."

"Yeah. She told me. But she said you tried."

I almost choked on a piece of tripe. I decided to play to Ratso's ego. All friendship aside, I needed his help.

"Okay. So I tried. But I didn't get anywhere. You know me. If I had access to hook-and-ladder truck number four-oh-seven and a heavy-metal *pisang*, I'd probably try to sodomize the Statue of Liberty."

"What's a *pisang?*"

"Means 'banana' in Malay."

We ate in silence for a while.

Finally, I said to Ratso, "Okay. Here's what I want. Find this out from Carmen: Was her adoptive father an alcoholic?"

"All right," said Ratso disgustedly, "but I'm getting tired of all this cryptic bullshit—the grasshopper game, your doubts and hints and warnings about Carmen, your paranoid behavior about the gas leak. You don't trust me anymore. You keep everything to yourself. You've been working full tilt on this case for quite a while now, and you're still nowhere as far as I can see."

I took out a cigar, went quickly through the prenuptial arrangements, and lighted it slowly and carefully.

"You know," said Ratso, with something close to dismay in his voice, "sometimes I wonder. What fucking detective school did you go to, Sherlock?"

I took a few leisurely puffs on the cigar before I picked up the check.

"Elementary, my dear Ratso," I said. "Elementary."

54

"No, I didn't know that Elvis never played to an empty seat, Cleve, but look where it got him."

It was later that afternoon, and a squall had blown up across the city. I'd taken time off from watching the rain with the cat to call Cleve back. Now one end of the blower was at the loft, and the other end was connected to the third ring of Saturn.

"All I'm saying is, it wouldn't hurt you to take a gig every once in a while. You've got a lot of fans out there, big guy. Let 'em know you're still alive."

I smiled grimly. Maybe my fans knew something I didn't know.

"Yeah," I said, "but fans like dead stars better than live ones. Lenny Bruce, Judy Garland, and Elvis all died on the throne, and Jim Morrison in the bathtub, and they have more fans than anyone except Wayne Newton, and he refuses steadfastly to go anywhere near a bathroom because he senses his own mortality."

"Kinkster," said Cleve, "you're running on here a little. You're not being rational."

"That's because I don't like to be called 'big guy.'"

"Well, you're being very juvenile, talking crazy. I just want you to listen to this. I've got a great idea."

I didn't like the fact that Cleve appeared to be patronizing me when I was the one who was supposed to be patronizing him. I had to admit, however, that he sounded pretty lucid.

"I could be a killer agent," he said.

"That's what I'm afraid of."

"I could book you on a tour of Texas. They love you down there, Kinkster."

"To paraphrase Bessie Smith, 'It's no disgrace to come from Texas. It's just a disgrace to have to go back there.' "

"We'll call it 'The Kinky Experience.' We'll get Jerry Retzloff and Lone Star beer behind it. We'll make T-shirts that say 'I Put a Lip-lock on a Longneck and Had a Kinky Experience—Texas Tour '89.' What do you think?"

I didn't know which I found more unsavory—the name of the tour, or the slogan on the T-shirt. At least the numerals at the end of the whole megillah weren't " '88."

"We can do it, baby!" Cleve shouted in a slightly unnerving fashion. "You and me against the world!"

"What about Helen Reddy?" I asked.

"She'll open for you," he said.

"Cleve—"

"I'll get to work on it now. 'The Kinky Experience.' 'The *Kinky* Experience.' " He said the phrase several more times, and each time his intonation became a little more frightening. At least, I thought, he hadn't reached that dangerous, terminally monstro-wigged condition where the patient unconsciously rhymes things all the time.

"Okay, Cleve. Good luck. Stay in touch."

"You won't regret it, Kinkster," he said, with a desperate quality in his voice that made me almost certain that I would. I started to cradle the blower, but Cleve, apparently, had more to tell me.

"Mickey says it's time to go. Give a little pat to the cat—hat—rat."

55

I stayed in all that weekend, but it wasn't quite as monastic an experience as it sounds. Saturday night I went dancing. You don't always have to go out to go dancing. Sometimes you can just go up.

That's what I did.

I walked up one flight of stairs, knocked on a door, and there stood Winnie Katz looking receptive, radiant, and ravishing. If heterosexuality was an accident, I felt like I'd just been T-boned by the *Sunset Limited*. How Winnie felt, of course, I couldn't say. But she did smile when she told me to park my cigar at the door.

It wasn't quite as sperm of the moment as it sounds. That morning Winnie'd been coming into the building with one of her girls and I'd been walking out carrying about four tons of cat shit in a large plastic tray. It was not an especially romantic encounter, I remember thinking at the time, but romance is so often not what we think it is, who can ever tell? The net result was that I dumped a grotesquely large amount of cat litter in the dumpster but did not return to the loft empty-handed. Winnie'd said if I had nothing to do I should drop by later that night. That was how I happened to be parking my cigar at the door of a lovely lesbian's loft, the occupant, now standing to one side, staring at me with an almost scientific curiosity, as if I were a rare specimen of a vanishing breed of colorful tropical fish that only thrived in some distant lagoon in Borneo. There were other fish in Borneo, I thought—big-ger and more dangerous fish—but why let them ruin a pleasant, platonic Saturday night?

I crossed the threshold.

None of Winnie's girls were there. Only one girl. And that was Winnie. She took my hand and showed me around the place. Soft music was playing from somewhere. We had the whole dance studio to ourselves, like Adam and Eve in the Garden of Eden trying to make up their minds whether the fruit was forbidden or merely tedious. The lights were suggestively low.

"Do you dance?" she asked.

"No," I said, "but I know Tommy Tune."

"He's not gonna help you much tonight, but I will."

What followed, a dance lesson of sorts, began rather awkwardly and asexually, yet ended in a moist and dreamy embrace. Many thoughts ran through my mind. The last time I'd been up to Winnie's loft I'd had to step over a dead Colombian. This time, I reflected, I might've had to step over something even stranger. I didn't know what it said about a man to be so attracted to a lesbian, but there wasn't time for me to call Dr. Charles Ansell and ask.

I kissed her tentatively at first, like a guy somewhere in Alabama making love for the first time with his cousin. I caught a look at her eyes before she closed them. They were as big as Susan B. Anthony silver dollars. Then we kissed more passionately.

"You're the first person," she said, "who's made my knees tremble since I was twelve years old." It was very flattering.

We drifted over to a bedroom and sat down on a tofu mattress. It looked like the same one I'd killed a Colombian on the year before. That was about the most comfortable thing you could do on a tofu mattress. He was the only man I'd ever killed in my life, and I was pleasantly surprised to find how little sleep I was losing over it. Of course, I didn't *sleep* on a tofu matress. It had been self-defense, but that wouldn't have made too much difference anyway. As I've often pointed out, you have to kill two people in New York before anybody notices.

On an old black-and-white TV set in the corner Humphrey Bogart was talking to Ingrid Bergman. Winnie went over to the set and turned the volume up a little. Then she came back and sat down next to me on the tofu mattress, taking my hand and holding it in her lap. She looked at me and smiled a smile that was almost heartbreaking in its innocence. Then her eyes drifted back to the flickering image of Humphrey Bogart smoking a cigarette.

"I've never seen this before," she said. "Is it *Casablanca?*"

It was two nights after I'd become the first person Winnie Katz had ever seen *Casablanca* with that I got another mysterious phone call from a kraut. I could tell by the way he rolled his *r*'s when he said the words "Herr Friedman." It was hard to determine if it was the same guy who'd called to tell me Ratso was dead. All Orientals look the same to you, all krauts sound the same to me.

To make a long and rather painful story short, the guy claimed to have information concerning the whereabouts of John Morgan. This, of course, I doubted. The guy wanted to meet me that night at a certain place and time I won't bother you with, to give me the information. This, of course, I suspected to be a trap.

The 88 organization, or whatever it was called, if it existed at all, had to comprise a small group of rather geriatric bad sports who refused to admit that they'd lost the war. No doubt they had the funds to recruit the occasional young skinhead or neo-Nazi lunatic along the way, but their hopes for taking over the world could probably be postmarked Fat Chance, Arkansas. This did not mean, however, that they would hesitate to kill a few more people in the glorious, mindless pursuit of their lost and hopeless cause.

I did not wish to become one of those people. I wanted to live another day so I could argue with Ratso. But it was a chance I had to take.

I noted the time and place of the assignation, told the kraut voice I'd be there, and cradled the blower. Then I called Rambam, Boris, and Sergeant Cooperman, told them each about the mysterious call (Cooperman was the least happy with this information), gave them the details of time and place, and cradled the blower three more times. I took a few cigars for the road, grabbed my hat and coat, and left the cat in charge.

Then I went to the place and waited for the time.

Time passes rather slowly when you're waiting for a mysterious kraut who you feel almost certain is not going to show up, but who you know, if he does, is going to try to kill you.

I can't say nothing happened. I'm sure, while we waited, many things did. Generations of Italian immigrants arrived on our shores, worked their way through life in the inner city, and moved out to the suburbs. A child playing with a paper boat in a gutter probably had time to grow up to be Lord Jim. Somewhere in New York a guy got a table in a restaurant.

Down the block in the gloom I was barely able to make out the shape of a car parked on the side of the street. This I took to be Cooperman, but I suppose it could've been Rambam or Boris as well. It never moved, and I couldn't tell if anyone was in it. Whoever it was, he was doing a pretty fair impersonation of a parked car.

It was a cold, foggy night, drizzling on and off. A good night to kill someone, as they go. Once I thought I saw a shadow moving along the side of a nearby building. Another time I heard hoarse shouting that sounded like it might've been in Russian. It wasn't guttural enough to be German, and it didn't much sound like the kind of English you'd hear in Texas. I crouched down and listened intently for a while until I realized it was two cab drivers yelling at each other.

A few people walked rather close to where I was standing, but if one of them was a Nazi he kept it pretty much to himself. Besides, the party I was looking for was not a three-hundred-pound woman, a man with a turban, or the young Negro who had just passed by with his shoelaces untied, his hat on sideways, and a handful of gold watches. Racists came in all sizes and colors, I thought, but you could count on Nazis at least to always be white.

After standing in the cold for what seemed like an eternity but was probably only a little under an hour and a half, Rambam stepped out of the darkness, waved, and shouted that he'd see me back at Vandam. Then the lights on the parked car came on, and it rolled up the street in my direction. When it came to a stop, I could see Cooperman and Fox in the car. Cooperman waved me over to the sidewalk. I lit a cigar and walked over to the car just as Cooperman chucked the butt of a dead Gauloise onto the curb. Fox's face was sneering like a cheerful Halloween mask.

"Sorry, fellas," I said, as I rubbed my hands together in the cold. "False alarm."

Cooperman pushed his hat back on his head and rubbed his forehead with his hand in a gesture of frustration. He lit another Gauloise.

"Tex," he said in a tired and world-weary voice, "a wise man once said, 'When baiting a trap with cheese, always leave enough room for the mouse.'"

57

I didn't own a mouse but I had a cat, and the cat was sitting on my lap when Rambam came through the door of the loft later that night with the puppet head in his hand.

"Nice domestic scene," he said.

"Don't rub it in."

"You feelin' all right?"

"What are you, a doctor?"

Rambam shot me a strange look, and if I hadn't known better I would've thought there was pity in his eyes. He set his black knapsack down on the couch, mentioned some errands he had to run, and headed for the door.

"I'll be back to check on you later," he said.

"We'll be here."

When Rambam had left I checked my travel alarm clock on the desk and noticed that it was pushing midnight. For some reason the loft seemed strangely empty and vulnerable now. Maybe the cat was just a cat. Maybe I was alone.

Suddenly, I felt nuts, paranoid, inordinately out of line with the other ducks. Strange thoughts came into my mind. How well did I really know Washington Ratso? What if someone had blown up his car for an altogether different reason, totally unrelated to me? And what about the gas leak and the two mysterious kraut phone calls? If these weren't the work of some far-flung member of 88, there was only one other possibility. And I didn't think I liked it at all.

Clearly, either the pieces of the John Morgan puzzle would have to come together soon, or I was in great danger of going to pieces myself. I looked at the phones. Whom could I call? Dr. Bock? Dr. Ansell? Dr. Ruth? I would've gotten up to get a shot of whatever snake piss happened to be around, but I didn't want to disturb the cat.

Not that I wasn't already somewhat disturbed myself. But people who love cats learn to think of the cat first and themselves second. Albert Schweitzer, who was left-handed, had a cat who always liked to sleep on his left arm. This forced Schweitzer to write much of his diary and many of his prescriptions with his right hand, which is why they remain almost illegible to this day. There is also a well-known story about Muhammad waking up at dawn to go to mosque and finding his cat sound asleep on the sleeve of his robe. Because of faulty record-keeping in those days, we do not know if it was his left sleeve or his right sleeve. All we know is that he took out his knife, cut the sleeve off his robe, and slipped out of it without awakening the cat. Possibly some of the other Arabs kidded him that morning at mosque about the appearance of his robe, but guys like Muhammad and Jesus were never very big in their sartorial area anyway. Of course, Ratso wasn't much in his sartorial area, and he hated cats. But Jesus loved cats. But then Jesus loved everybody. What did that prove?

This is the way the mind of a detective works, I thought. This is the way he sorts things out.

Then there was Winston Churchill's cat, Jock. During most of his later adult life Churchill refused to eat until Jock was seated at the table, and would not sleep until Jock was in bed with him. Maybe I was only a *little* out of line with the other ducks.

The phones rang.

The cat twitched an ear, and I reached across for the blower on the left.

It was Ratso.

"So aside from carrying on an affair with a lesbian,

having an agent who's booking you out of a mental hospital, and refusing to tell me what the grasshopper game is, what else is going on?" he asked.

It's hard to keep a secret in New York.

I smoked a cigar, stroked the cat, and had a long and oddly comforting talk with Ratso. We discussed everything from Hitler to hockey and back to Hitler again. We talked about some of the cases we'd solved together in the past, some of the exciting times we'd had, some of the close calls. For a moment it almost felt like it was all over. Ratso and I were o-l-d, sitting on the porch of some bungalow in the Shalom Retirement Village, resting up between shuffleboard games.

This sensation, fortunately, did not linger long. The conversation hit a jarring note when Ratso told me that Carmen had told him unequivocally that no one in her family had ever been an alcoholic. I said, "That fits." Ratso said, "What fits?" I said, "I can't tell you yet." Ratso said something that was quite unprintable.

"I'll let you know soon," I said.

"Promise?"

"As my friend Fred Katz says, 'My word of honor as a furrier.' "

We hung up in our normal state of rancor.

I got up, which greatly irritated the cat—who probably didn't realize that I couldn't go on sitting there for the rest of my life—went into the bedroom, got out of my clothes, and put on my sarong and my T-shirt with the picture of Elvis shaking hands with President Nixon on the occasion of Elvis being made a drug-enforcement deputy. I may have played before a lot of empty seats in my life, I reflected, but I was doing better than either of them.

I didn't know when Rambam was coming back, and I wasn't going to wait up for him. Just before he'd left I'd given him an extra key so the puppet head and I could get some sleep. But, as I Indian-wrestled with Morpheus, I wondered what or who it was that John Morgan had stumbled upon that might've placed his life and mine in the danger I now believed us to be.

There was a big fish out there somewhere. It was deadly and it was deep. And it was lurking just beyond the shadowy waterline of my vision.

A train roars through the night and the fog. The cowboy stars stare with empty eyes into the lonely attic. Faces crowded together on the train. Eyes like black smudges against the black forest night.

A wall of a laboratory consisting of a solid mass of human eyeballs. A lampshade, upon close inspection, appears to be made of the stretched skin of human beings.

It's the kind of dream that is so close to reality that it doesn't make any sense at all.

Heaven can't hear this train. Railroad ties can't bind the hopeless wound it cuts in the world. This is the train that Frank and Jesse James cannot stop.

It runs like a silent screaming souvenir of evil that no one will save and few will remember. Only the cowboy stars who shudder against the wall as the wind sweeps the little attic.

The train stops at a station on the way to eternity. There is a debonair young man with shiny black boots and a space between his teeth. He is shouting a strange word in a strange tongue. The word sounds like *"Zwillinge! Zwillinge!"*

The children are walking away from the train in twos, like a little, human Noah's Ark.

A terrible page torn clean from the Old Testament and thrown to the wind.

Sometimes a songwriter has a dream in which he hears the words and the music and he knows, even though he's dreaming, that they've come together right. When he wakes up, the first thing he does is rush for a pen and paper to get it all down just like it was in the dream. He acts with great intensity, because he knows from experience that sometimes it's still there and sometimes it's gone.

The sensation I felt was an equal mixture of exhilaration and frustration. I had it and I didn't want to lose it. It had to do with "the greatest genius the world has ever known." It had to do with Morgan's pictures of the old man in the jungle and the young man with shiny black boots at the train, both of whom had a space between their teeth. It had to do with the vision of the two little native boys with blue eyes I saw in my delirium when I was receiving the tattoo that I now hoped to God would protect my soul.

Suddenly, it all came together very vividly. The music in the dream was of a heavily Dopplered, distorted, Wagnerian, country-rock flavor. It did not sound like it would cross over. The lyrics were sort of a subliminal rap of all the evil murmurings in the world.

Crazy as dreams can sometimes be, I knew in my heart that this one would still be true when I opened my eyes. I knew where the big fish was. Not only that, I knew his name.

But a new sensation was now rolling over me like waves of terror. I felt or saw or somehow sensed a presence in the room near the bed. A man in a peaked cap. For a moment I thought that a doorman from the Helmsley Palace had wandered into my bedroom.

Another wave of terror crashed into the dream. Now I was looking through the eyes of the brilliant, hard-living journalist Piers Akerman. Piers had been born in New Guinea, and what I was now experiencing seemed to have a very primitive, cannibalistic ambience about it. Ambience is only important in two places: dreams and restaurants. If this was a dream, it was becoming almost as unpleasant as what passes for reality. If it was a restaurant, it was time to tell the waiter to· eighty-six the raspberry sorbet and drop the hatchet.

But it was not a restaurant, and it was apparently not entirely a dream. I was Piers Akerman and I was floating somewhere out to sea in a big storm. The vessel that was carrying me looked and felt uncomfortably like McGovern's couch.

An Irish buttocks the size of a Liberian-registered tanker seemed to loom over me like the long-forgotten playground shadow of a childhood bully. I was not Piers Akerman. I was myself. I was in great danger.

I opened my eyes.

Someone was indeed standing there. It took a second or two for my dream-frazzled orbs to adjust to the gloomy room. Then I saw who it was.

It was not McGovern.

It was Wilhelm Stengal.

59

I felt like I'd just gotten a wake-up call in hell. Maybe I *was* in hell, because Stengal, I knew, was dead: He even looked a little dead. Like death lightly microwaved. And if I wasn't in hell, what was Stengal doing in New York?

Of course, normally I did not think of hell as a geographic place. But fear is a funny thing. Sometimes it'll make a Catholic schoolchild out of you. For about sixteen seconds there it had me reaching for my rosary.

Then logic kicked in.

Like Descartes, I deduced something very basic. There is an elderly Nazi standing in my bedroom, therefore I am.

I took a closer look at Stengal's hat. It was better than looking at his face. There was a silver skull-and-crossbones on the front of the hat. I remembered vaguely that I'd seen hats with emblems such as this in old World War II movies on late-night television. They were worn by some kind of SS death-squad guys. But the war was over. Almost fifty years had passed. It seemed incredible that so much had happened in the world since then and that so little had changed inside Wilhelm Stengal's head.

Suspended between the dark cap and a black shirt was a face that I now gazed upon with something near to a-mazement. It was shocking in appearance. It looked like a cold, wrinkled mask of white, withering, genocidal hatred.

Then he smiled.

It was charming in a rather diseased way, but the longer you looked at that smile, the more horrific it became. Many years ago it might've won over a *Fräulein* or two, but now it was only the wax lips of an old man forever smiling when the obvious intent was a rather sinister sneer. That, or the whole world was upside down. One possibility was about as likely as the other.

Against the black of his shirt was a red armband with a black swastika set in a white background. Nice color scheme.

How Stengal had survived the fire storm on East

Eighty-sixth Street, I did not know. Maybe the bunker had a secret emergency exit. Maybe Satan watched over child molesters and old Nazis. Possibly the bunker was fire-proofed. As Smokey the Bear always says, "Never leave the site of a campfire until you're sure the crispy critter is fried just the way you like it."

Stengal had the Luger out again, and this time I wasn't taking any bets against his chances of squeezing off a successful shot. His eyes were shining like moonlight on the Rhine. He loved his work. He was an old Nazi, and I was becoming rapidly resigned to the fact that I might never get to be an ancient Jewish person and move to the land of my people, Miami.

We watched each other's eyes, if not with trust, at least with understanding. It was almost as if we were savoring the moment. For we, along with John Robert Morgan, shared a monstrous secret.

A chill passed through the room encompassing both of us. It was too much power, too much history, too much responsibility for the mind of man to feel comfortable with. Stengal, like the other Nazis, I'm sure, felt he was "not responsible." Not responsible for trains, smoke, or children. Not responsible for man-made lime-laden valleys of death where countless thousands were buried together alive or almost alive. Not responsible for the Jews. Not responsible for the Gypsies. Not responsible for sailing a paper boat down a river of blood or watching the sun set over a hill of human hair.

Who *was* responsible? The Red Baron? Hansel and Gretel?

I could tell, looking into Stengal's eyes in the half-darkness, that he now felt responsible for something. He felt responsible for keeping the secret. I, I'm sure he knew, felt responsible for telling the secret to the world.

Neither of us probably knew exactly where John Morgan was. But we both knew one thing. John, while deep in the jungles of Borneo, had indeed stumbled upon a white tiger with blue eyes.

The secret was that the tiger walked on two legs.

I looked from the gun, to the swastika, to the skull-and-crossbones, to the eyes. The eyes had it.

As I searched for a hint, even a glint, of humanity, I found them empty as an office building in Texas. They shone like a glass skyscraper in the winter sun, with that cold, brittle light that emanates from the Dallas of the soul.

As I watched, Stengal's eyes began to blink rapidly. As Ratso would say, not a good sign. He was blinking rapidly and I was thinking rapidly, and this went on for about seven years.

Then he reached his left hand over to steady his right wrist. Every muscle in my body tensed.

His face was as somber as an old German clock, and as he blinked, the wrinkles at the corners of his eyes seemed to tick away the seconds of my life. Then, suddenly, the nervous blinking stopped, and the old man's eyes opened wide as ovens.

"*Heute, Deutschland,*" he shouted, "*Morgen, die ganze Welt!*"

"Hold the weddin', pal," I said, in what I hoped was a soothing, rational voice. "We're both after the same thing." This, of course, was a fatuous lie. I didn't feel, however, it was the kind of thing that, if Stengal were to blow my brains out, Saint Peter would hold against me.

"Once we find Morgan," I continued in an even tone, "then we can settle our differences. As Ted Kennedy said, 'We'll cross that bridge when we come to it.'"

"*Juden raus!*" Stengal roared, waving the Luger wildly. "*Juden raus!*"

I sensed that he wanted me to leave. I also sensed that he wasn't going to give me the chance. I didn't have my German–English dictionary by my bedside, so I was flying by Jewish radar in more ways than one. He seemed to be growing rather frighteningly irrational and agitated, which rarely bodes well for you when you're sitting third row center to a Luger.

"I'm not here alone," I said. This was patently false, and we both knew it. I could almost hear my voice echo through the empty loft. I was trying to stall Stengal in the slim hope that Rambam might return in time to save my life for the fourth time this month. Maybe the Baby Jesus was trying to tell me something. But Rambam, I knew, when he went on an "errand," might not be back for a week.

"You won't get away with this, Stengel." I was pulling out all the clichés, or, rather, fear was pulling them out of me. I knew the likelihood was that Stengal *would* get away with it, and Stengal, for his part, didn't seem to really give a damn.

They would find me, I suspected, many months later. The cat and I would probably be in rather advanced stages of decomposition. Maybe a Jehovah's Witness who was overly zealous would come to the door one day and smell us. "Zealous" and "smell us," I thought to myself, made a rather nice rhyme scheme. I also realized that that was exactly the kind of nonsense that probably cluttered the minds of most men seconds before their deaths. It probably also cluttered the minds of the Clutter family. Well, there was nothing to do but think crazy thoughts. Any attempt at vocalization seemed only to rile Stengal, and that was certainly to be avoided.

It was funny, I reflected, but McGovern and I had set up the man-in-trouble hotline for precisely this purpose. So that if anything happened to us, a Jehovah's Witness who was zealous wouldn't come to the door and smell us. McGovern and I called each other on a fairly regular basis, opening the conversation with the acronym "MIT . . . MIT . . . MIT."

If you lived alone in a major city in North America, you needed the MIT hotline. In a fraction of a second I worked out what everybody else in my life would think if Stengal were to pull the trigger, then slip quietly out the fire escape. They would all, of course, get my answering machine. Ratso would assume, when I didn't return the call, that I was miffed about something. That would miff Ratso, and it'd be a while before he called again. Decomposition would begin. Winnie would call, and when she didn't hear back from me, she'd assume I had a fear of intimacy or something. She'd harden her attitude toward men. Maybe after a few weeks she'd tell Dr. Bock about it. Decomposition would continue. A sample call might be from my friend Sal Lorello, who ran a limo service out of Chappaqua, New York and who'd once acted as road manager for me when Cleve was busy listening to Hank Williams records. Sal might say, "Okay, Kinky Man, I guess you're out raising hell tonight. Call me when you get in." He might or might not say, "*Ciao.*" When I didn't call Sal back, he'd watch a few Giants games, meet a few new beautiful women, then, eventually, get around to checking back on me again. This time he'd say, "Kinky Man! Where are you? Okay, you must be in Texas. I wish I was with you. Tell your dad and Marcie hello for me." Decomposition would progress rather alarmingly. The lack of adequate heating in the loft might retard it somewhat, but you couldn't really count on something like that. Cooperman might even call just to rattle my cage. I kept no regular hours, so if he called me late at night he might just assume, as others would, that

I was out on a tear. He might say something patronizing, like, "Tex? You keepin' your powder dry?" Decomposition.

Actually, by the time I saw Stengal's index finger tighten, I was almost looking forward to it. Decomposition was probably preferable to a lot of things. One of them was looking at Stengal's eyes.

Then the cat jumped on the bed.

Stengal shot an irritated glance at the cat, then took two steps closer. I reached out and patted the cat on the head. Stengal shifted the Luger to his left hand. It looked like he'd had about enough. He raised his right hand high in the air. I couldn't decide if it was absurd or terrifying, but it was clearly Stengal's final statement. A Nazi salute.

"*Sieg Heil!*" he shouted. "*Heil* Hitler!"

The cat looked at Stengal, then looked at me questioningly. One of the most difficult things we ever have to do in life is explain a Nazi salute to a cat. I figured I'd wait until she got a little older.

I wondered very fleetingly what the girl in the peach-colored dress would say when she called my answering machine. Stengal shifted the Luger back to his right hand, steadied his wrist, and took aim.

Just as Rambam roared through the door and hit him like the Rockaway shuttle, he pulled the trigger.

61

I figured it was about time I got out of bed. The cat was nowhere to be seen. There wasn't a hell of a lot to be seen, in fact, as I stumbled through the gloom and made a determined effort to find the light switch. I could hear Rambam and Stengal struggling somewhere on the floor between the far side of the bed and the wall. The acrid smell of the gun shot in the small room was powerful enough for even my beezer to pick up on. Just as I hit the lights, a second shot rang out.

I looked across the room, but my vision was obscured briefly by the bed. Then Rambam stood up with the Luger in his hand and something approaching a little Charles Whitman smile twitching on his lips.

I walked across the room on tiptoe for some reason, remembering as I did that that was the curious way John Morgan often walked. I stood at the foot of the bed and peered over the far side of it. Stengal's waxen face was just visible. One eye was gone. Well, it wasn't really gone. It was somewhere deep in the base of his skull looking around like a child in the Black Forest at the dark and twisted branches that extended through his gray matter department. I couldn't be sure what, if anything, Stengal himself was seeing, but one look at his body was enough for me. I was as close as I ever wanted to literally finding a Nazi under my bed.

Rambam, however, was excited by something. He motioned me to come closer, then lifted Stengal's left arm to reveal a tear in his shirt that had been incurred during the struggle.

"See that jagged scar under his armpit?"

"Yeah," I said in a thick voice. It isn't everybody, at four o'clock in the morning, who gets to see a scar under a Nazi's armpit.

"That's where SS men always tattooed their blood-types. After the war, they often had the tattoos removed, sometimes somewhat clumsily, to hide their identity. It was in case they were wounded in battle. Helped the doctors in giving them transfusions. Too bad Stengal removed his tattoo. Maybe we could've helped him."

Rambam smiled.

I walked into the other room, poured two double shots out of a new bottle of Jack Daniel's, downed one of them, found a cigar, lit it, refilled my bull's horn, and waited for Rambam to come out of the killing fields.

Moments later he came in, pitched the Luger onto the kitchen table, and lifted his glass.

"Here's to the occupants of Muranowska Seven," he said.

"Here's to the Chicago Seven."

"Very funny. Muranowska Seven was the address of the command bunker at the Warsaw Ghetto."

"A fairly obscure toast, but I'll drink to it."

"*L'chaim.*"

We killed the shots, and I paced back and forth a little in the kitchen, smoking the cigar and figuring out what the hell to do next. It was an unusual American, I thought, who could make a toast "to life" only moments after splicing a man, even if the stiff was a Nazi. But then, who among us is without his little foibles and inconsistencies?

"Glossing over the fact," I said, "that you saved my life, what purpose did it serve to kill the old bastard? He might've been holding back some information on Morgan. Maybe the authorities would've wanted to talk to him. You didn't have to ice the geek."

"The gun went off in the struggle," Rambam said with an amiable grin. "That's my story, and I'm sticking to it."

"Of course, I have to call Cooperman," I said. The thought was not a particularly pleasant one, but it was nicer than the notion of hiding a Nazi under your bed during the advanced stages of decomposition.

"You could make German sausage out of him," said Rambam as he poured himself another shot. "Keep him in the freezer along with your five-alarm Lone Star Cafe chili."

"No, I don't think so. There's two occupational groups

that I never wish to see in action: politicians and sausage-stuffers."

Rambam thought about it for a moment and shrugged his shoulders. "Hell of an idea," he said.

I walked over to the kitchen window and opened it a couple of inches to let in some air but not far enough for the cat to fall out. People say cats won't fall out of windows, and if they do they always land on their feet. If that's what you think, you ought to talk to Joel Siegel. His cat took a nosedive off the sixteenth floor onto Riverside Drive. The results were not pleasant.

I walked back over to the desk and called Cooperman.

"This better be fucking good, Tex," he said.

"Not to worry."

When I cradled the blower, I checked the clock and walked back into the kitchen area of the loft. It was four-thirty of a chilly Tuesday morning in March of the year of our Lord 1989, if you followed the Gregorian Calendar. If you followed the Jewish Calendar, it was the month of Adar in the year 5750. Only a minor discrepancy in the dates. I'm sure they could work it out.

"Cooperman coming?" Rambam asked. I nodded. He was now seated at the kitchen table, upon which rested the cat and the Luger. Rambam picked up the Luger.

"Why don't you try playing Russian roulette with it?" I asked.

Rambam ignored me. He put down the Luger, walked over to the sink, washed his hands thoroughly with soap and hot water, dried them off, went back over to the table, and picked up the Luger again. He took out a handkerchief, walked back into the bedroom. The cat watched him disappear into the bedroom, then looked at me. I shrugged my shoulders.

I stoked up the espresso machine and put it in gear, and soon Rambam, the cat, and I were sitting around the kitchen table, Lugerless, sipping espresso and waiting for

Cooperman. All except the cat, of course. The cat didn't like espresso. It's an acquired taste. Rambam was making loud mewing noises to the cat. The cat didn't much like that either.

"Well," I said, "isn't this nice?"

"The fucking Bobbsey Twins in the country," said Rambam, as he sipped his espresso.

"I've got to call Ratso," I said, a bit uncomfortably. "I want him to tell Carmen for me."

"Tell Carmen what?"

I looked over to the window. I could hear the sounds of a tire squealing against the curb and two car doors slamming.

"Tell Carmen that we've found her father," I said.

Cooperman was not pleased. He tried to conceal his irritation, but I could tell.

"You don't fuckin' discriminate, do you, Tex?" he shouted from the bedroom.

I had the right to remain silent, and I did.

Cooperman came out into the living room. By now the loft was a hive of activity. Technicians were measuring the angle of the bullet in the headboard of my bed. Technicians were photographing the body. Technicians were dusting the Luger. I considered asking one of them to take a look at some of the problems I was having with my old black-and-white television set, but it was a little late for levity.

Fox and a burly party I'd never seen before were working over Rambam in a far corner of the loft. The discussion seemed to be throwing off a nice number of sparks. Fox was becoming more and more agitato. Rambam was coming up with a wide enough repertoire of hand gestures to have been directing traffic in Times Square. I couldn't tell if the influence was from the Jewish or the Italian side of the family, but as the conversation became more and more animated, it began to look like it might be the Italian.

A little after five in the morning Cooperman flew out of the bedroom like a large and extremely angry bee and started circling counterclockwise around my head. I was sitting at the kitchen table studying the leaves of my seventh espresso.

"Last year," he snarled, "we get a call to come over here and we extricate seven wasted Colombians. This time, we come over to your place and what do we find? A dead kraut!"

"I'm an equal-opportunity employer," I said.

Cooperman had a few choice words, then left in the direction of the stiff trailing more steam than a train pulling out of Grand Central. Fox drifted by and helped himself to a cup of espresso. When he walked back past me, he was holding his cup like a demitasse in an exaggeratedly effeminate fashion.

"You must tell me where you get your coffee," he said.

"When my lawyer gets here."

"You know, Tex, I know how you feel," Fox said with a razor-thin grin. "I lost my favorite uncle in a concentration camp."

"Sorry to hear it," I said as I set fire to the end of a cigar.

"Yeah, poor ol' Uncle Max." Fox took a sip of espresso, timing his delivery. "He was makin' the rounds one afternoon when he dropped his swagger stick. Prisoner jumped up and choked him to death." Fox chuckled like a rabid chipmunk.

"Sorry to hear it," I said.

Fox chuckled again and went back over to Rambam. Cooperman came out of the bedroom, went over to the desk, made a phone call, walked over to where I was sitting, pulled out a chair, and sat down across the table from me. He took a Gauloise out of his pack and, with a thoughtful and almost conciliatory expression in his eyes, lit it slowly with his Zippo.

"I don't know, Tex, what you've got yourself into this time. What with the disappearing broad at the Pierre Hotel two weeks ago, the unsolved bombing of your friend's car in Washington, the mysterious fire at the brownstone on East Eighty-sixth Street, and this elderly skell showing up in his Halloween suit—you're gettin' into an area that ain't really my beat. Maybe you need Interpol or Mr. Spock or somebody. I saved your ass at the Garden last year, but if this *ain't* a Halloween suit this stiff was wearin', I may not be able to always be around to hold your hand."

Cooperman stood up, killed the Gauloise, gave a sign to Fox, lit another Gauloise, and looked at me with a kind of tough wistfulness through the smoke.

"I know you admire Nero Wolfe," he said. "But just remember, Wolfe only arranged to have the *suspects* come to him. He didn't always have their goddamn dead *bodies* lying around his house."

As if on cue, two guys began carrying what used to be Stengal through the living room. He was wrapped up so you couldn't see him, but you could feel an evil aura almost pulsate from the body bag as they passed between the desk and the kitchen table.

"Get him outta here," Cooperman snarled, waving off the stiff like a guy passing on a hand of cards.

Not too much later, everyone else was gone, too. There were still things Cooperman wanted to talk to me and Rambam about, but that, apparently, was it for the night. It was a good thing too, because the sun was peeking in the window from the east.

I picked up the cat and carried her over to the couch, where both of us lay down to take a little power nap together. I didn't feel like walking all the way to the bedroom.

"Believe me, Ratso, Carmen's adoptive father was an SS man named Wilhelm Stengal. Probably since some time shortly after the war, he's been protecting a major Nazi fish who's been in hiding deep in the jungles of Borneo. No one would think to look there, and no one did until John Morgan, who was looking for him in South America, tumbled onto his true whereabouts."

It was ten o'clock Tuesday morning, A.P.N. (After Power Nap), when I finally got around to the rather unpleasant chore of calling Ratso. The cat, a lit cigar in an ashtray, and a cup of hot chocolate with mini-marshmallows were arrayed before me, perfectly positioned in true Hercule Poirot style between the two red telephones.

I was downshifting from a fairly steady diet of espresso, which will burn your brain cells out at almost the rate of Peruvian marching powder but is, of course, cheaper. The hot chocolate always seemed to go well with a cigar, and it was a welcome change from the ground Colombian fast lane. It was like stopping to smell the flowers, if your beezer could smell the flowers. If it couldn't, you could practice tonguing the mini-marshmallows out of the hot chocolate. Never know when it might come in handy. I tongued a few mini-marshmallows and listened to Ratso's incredulous, rodentlike tones.

"That's abso-fucking-lutely ridiculous," he said.

"Not when you consider that Stengal came to my loft last night and tried to kill me. Fortunately, Rambam walked in just at the time, and Stengal was killed. Gun went off in the struggle." I was almost beginning to believe the last part. It was starting to have a nice ring to it.

"You're kidding."

"I'm not kidding. Where's Carmen now?"

"She's still asleep."

"Okay, then pull your lips together for a minute and I'll explain. Carmen and her father kind of had a relationship like Patty Hearst and that guy—what was his name? Bocephus?"

"Bocephus?"

"You know. The guy that was head of the SLA."

"Oh, Cinque."

"You're welcome. But you see, she lived in fear of him, but for a long time he was all she knew. Stengal—"

"Bocephus? Jesus Christ."

"Stengal, according to Carmen, was an engineer from Europe, but what he really was, was a *chemical* engineer from Hitler's Germany, an SS man, and the keeper of a terrible secret that I will reveal to you at a later date. He knew about Zyklon-B derivatives, had a chemical lab set up in the basement of his brownstone, and he wasn't an alcoholic, so when Carmen told me she'd once heard her mother saying, 'Stay away from me, Bill. Don't come near me when you smell that way,' it either means he'd been working in a lab all day with extremely pungent chemicals and his wife was kind of a ball-busting, insensitive twit, or that he had a rather tertiary case of halitosis. Are you with me so far?"

"I read you, Bocephus."

"Carmen's mother called him Bill, so it was Wilhelm to William, William to Will, Will to Bill, or something along that order. Add to this the fact that when Carmen talked to me at this loft she kept wanting me to find *him* not *them*. She'd forgotten that her father was supposed to be missing too, because actually he wasn't. I now believe the abduction at the Pierre was a setup that didn't quite come off, and I know she was involved in setting up the skinhead attack on me. She was the only one, other than you, who knew when I was coming, when I was going, and had the time to do it. You don't get five skinheads out of Central Casting that fast. The attack was prearranged, and when you and I left your apartment, she called somebody, probably Stengal, to tip him off. That's the only way it could've happened. I don't blame her. She was under Stengal's powerful influence since she was a small girl. Adopting a Jewish child, keeping her original name, and turning her to his own purposes probably appealed to Stengal's perversity. Also it provided good cover for him.

"When you tell her about Stengal's death, break it to her gently, Ratso. I still want to talk to her about Morgan. Let's have dinner tomorrow night at the Derby. Bring Carmen if she wants to come. I'll fill you in on the rest of it."

"Okay," said Ratso. "I'll wake her now." His voice sounded different, like all at once he was immeasurably older.

I hung up the blower, patted the cat, took a sip of hot chocolate, leaned back in the chair, and puffed the cigar, and suddenly I felt very sorry for Ratso.

64

I had lunch at an all-day dim sum place in Chinatown with Mike Simmons, who was on the wagon again and therefore a rather stultifying luncheon companion. For all I know, he probably thought the same of me. Gone were the golden days of innocence and truth when Mike would vomit on the head of the woman at the next table and I would threaten to stick my fork in the waitress's eye. My excuse was that I only had chopsticks. Simmons's excuse was that it was no fun to go around walking on your knuckles in southern California, where he was now spending most of his time, because everybody did there. He proceeded to give me many reasons why he did not like southern California and why he missed New York. I empathized.

It is a fact of life today that New Yorkers are fast moving out of New York to live in other parts of the country, and, upon arrival in Buttocks, Texas, or Plymouth Rock, or wherever they wind up, they never stop bitching about the absence of things that they never gave a damn about when they lived in New York. While this does not endear them to the locals, it does make people begin to wonder what they might be missing by living in Buttocks, Texas. So they try to accommodate. The result is that today you can get a bagel in Texas, but you can't really get a *bagel* in Texas.

There is very little danger of the rest of the country becoming more like New York or New York becoming more like the rest of the country. That would be terrible. Soon someone would come up to you on a street in Manhattan and say, "Have a nice day," before they mugged you.

But the main result of this migration of New Yorkers is that people in small towns and communities throughout mid-America are becoming ever-so-slowly aware of attitudes, values, and a unique cultural upbringing that probably is totally foreign to their own. Their growth and enlightenment is interesting to note. Now we can all sit back and wait for the fifties to catch up with them.

Unfortunately, the eighties had caught up with me, and they were doing a pretty good job of pulling my coattails.

Somewhere between the dream I'd had the night before and my waking up staring into the barrel of Stengel's Luger, I'd known there was a call I had to make. It was already a lifetime too late, so I didn't figure a few more hours were going to make a hell of a lot of difference. Nevertheless, as soon as I got back to the loft, I sat down at the desk and picked up the blower.

My brother, Roger, who works in our nation's capital, had once given me the name of a friend who held a high-level position in the Justice Department. His name was Nathan Gabriel, and he was involved with the Office of Special Investigations. I dialed Information and got the number. I extracted a cigar from Sherlock Holmes's head, lopped the end off in the guillotine, set fire to it with a kitchen match, took a healthy puff, and called Gabriel.

"This is not a secure line," was the first thing he told me after he identified himself.

I told Gabriel, outlandish as it may have seemed, what I believed to be the truth.

"Very unlikely," he said. "I've been to Brazil and seen the dental X rays and other evidence two years ago. The root-canal work he had done shortly before he died. His personal diary written in his own hand. Of course, we have had and continue to have some terrific sightings. He's been seen playing in a marimba band in Las Vegas. He's been seen dealing cards in Atlantic City. He's been spotted on the staff of several major hospitals in New York and Philadelphia. But frankly, he's dead."

It took some time, but I gave Gabriel everything I had. All the personal, firsthand evidence, unusual as it was, to bolster my strong belief that he was wrong. When I finished, there was a long, reflective pause on his end of the line. When he spoke again, there was a different tone in his voice.

"What you say is very interesting. I don't know what

we can do about it, but there are those who might wish to take action. I'll see that the information is passed on to the Israelis, the West Germans, and the Simon Wiesenthal Institute in Vienna.

"Of course, you are not alone in your view that he's still alive. There are thousands of people in a group they call 'the Candles' who believe him to be such a clever fiend as to be quite capable of fabricating his own death. The group is also known sometimes as the '*Zwillinge* Organization.' "

I almost dropped my cigar. It was the word I'd heard in my dream.

"*Zwillinge*," I said. "What does that word mean?"

"*Zwillinge?*" said Nathan Gabriel. "*Zwillinge* is the German word for 'twins.' "

At around nine-thirty on Wednesday night, I was sitting at the bar in the Derby Restaurant chatting it up with a very skinny woman with convex breasts who was about nine feet three inches tall. I was drinking a Carta Blanca and smoking a Romeo y Julieta cigar that said "Habana" on it and had been sent to me from Switzerland by a lady named Rocky. Andrew's son, also very inventively named Andrew, was behind the bar serving the skinny broad a large number of straight shots of a thick yellow fluid that I hoped wasn't Galliano.

"This was Churchill's favorite cigar and Travis McGee's favorite beer," I said.

"Who's Churchill?" she wanted to know.

I was watching the door for Ratso, but so far I hadn't

had any terrific sightings, as Nathan Gabriel would say. I turned back to the woman.

"He's a high school in upstate New York," I said.

"Who's Travis McGee?" she wanted to know. I was beginning to get a little worried about Ratso.

"Look it up when you get home," I said. She downed the shot, and Andrew was rather hesitantly pouring her another one when Ratso walked in wearing slacks and a sport coat almost identical to the color of the fluid she was drinking. He looked like a slightly overstuffed canary who'd been eaten by the cat and lived to tell about it. He again had on the coonskin cap with the tail on it and with the little face affixed to the front. He signaled to me and walked directly to a booth in the front of the place. He was noticeably without Carmen. I wasn't greatly surprised.

As I got up to join Ratso at the table, the lady at the bar stood up, knocked back the shot in front of her, turned around, and looked down on me like I was a low-flying snail-darter.

"Who're you?" she wanted to know.

"I own this restaurant," I said.

I joined Ratso at the little booth, and it didn't take long for me to realize that he was going to be about as much fun as the lady at the bar.

"She's gone," he said.

"Carmen?"

"Who the fuck do you think?"

I motioned the waiter over and ordered a couple of stiff ones. When they arrived, we killed them in silence and ordered two more. The waiter was an older gentleman whom a former girlfriend had once told me had the nicest face she'd ever seen in her life. She'd never liked mine too much, of course, but that's the way it goes. I was better off without her, anyway. She was pretty neurotic. Whenever I'd offered her a piece of gum, she'd always asked for the second one from the top. She didn't want to take a piece that might have some "pocket juice" on it. I was blinded by love at the time, so I thought this was cute. I'd told Ratso about it once, however, and he'd said it was the most disgusting thing he'd ever heard in his life. Looking at the waiter's face as he brought the second round, I reflected that love may be grand and love may be blind, but the fear of getting pocket juice on a piece of wrapped gum should never be categorized as attractive behavior.

We ordered the meal, worked more slowly on the second round of drinks, and looked at each other. There was nothing I could really say to Ratso that would help. There are some things you never get over. You just get above.

"Face it, Rats, she was engaged to Morgan, sleeping with you, and coming on to me when it suited her. She wasn't very loyal to you or to John, and when Stengal got liquidated, she just bolted. There was nothing else she wanted here."

"I know," said Ratso.

"As my friend Alden Shuman says, 'She was one of those women who will stick with you through thick.'"

"I know," said Ratso. I could see that he didn't, but who the hell was I to talk? I'd gone around for five years thinking "pocket juice" was cute.

When the meal arrived, Ratso brightened somewhat, even to the point of asking me again what the grasshopper game was, and who was the big fish I'd been making veiled references to recently. I told him I'd discuss it with him after the meal.

It was Nero Wolfe's dictum never to discuss business during a meal, and besides, the big fish being who he was, I did not wish to discuss him while eating the Catch of the Day.

"It was the gap between his teeth that first put me on to him. The photographs that Morgan sent Carmen. One of them was of an old man in the jungle with a panama hat and a gap between his two front teeth. The skinheads later stole the photographs, but, like the gap in the Watergate tapes, the absence of something is sometimes more telling than its presence. I've done a little checking up, and it was one of the best-known features of the man."

The waiter had cleared the dinner plates, and Ratso and I were drinking coffee and sipping sambuca. Ratso also was busy attacking a piece of the Derby's dessert specialty, walnut-apple-pecan cake, which was roughly the size of his hat.

"In connection with that photograph, you'll remember, was a rather cryptic comment from Morgan to Carmen: 'Dr. Breitenbach, I presume.' That checks out as one of the four or five regular aliases he used. I've already told you, I believe, how and why I place the suspect in Borneo— Morgan's Land Rover being driven on the left-hand side of the jungle highway.

"What I think happened was this. Morgan was in South America, probably already on the trail of the suspect— remember the photo Carmen found in his apartment of the gap-toothed man?

"Morgan, like the pro that he was, ran into this Peace Corps volunteer down there, a guy named John Morgan from Cleveland, Ohio. The guy I know as John Morgan got hold of the Peace Corps kid's passport, identification papers, and even old photos of his parents, had them copied and maybe doctored a bit, and picked up what's known as a 'floating identity' he could use for himself. When the suspect fled to Borneo—he might've gone back and forth many times—Morgan wasn't far behind. That's where I met Morgan, naturally assuming he was who he said he was."

"This is all very circumstantial," Ratso said between large chompings of walnut-apple-pecan cake. "There are probably lots of old men hanging out in weird places with panama hats and gaps between their two front teeth. Where does it all lead?"

"Well, it didn't lead anywhere for a long time. The big fish was lurking at the very bottom of a very deep pool. All I could see was his shadow in the water. Then I started putting together some things that some people had told me. My friend Dylan's account of his malarial attack in the *ulu* when he was trying to run down the legend of the white tiger with the blue eyes. After seeing the tiger—obviously a malarial hallucination of some kind—he passed out. Upon awakening, he was surrounded by a group of native men, who, if he hadn't known better, he said, had looked at him and given him a Nazi salute. Of course, later Dylan wrote this off as a fevered vision just like the sighting of the tiger. The tiger might've been only in his mind, but the native men giving him the Nazi salute was for real.

"I ask you, Ratso, where did those Kenyah tribesmen learn a Nazi salute?"

"Maybe they watched late-night movies like the rest of us."

"I'm afraid they don't have Manhattan Cable in Borneo. In fact, no television at all, no VCR, no stereos, no McDonald's."

"That *is* primitive."

"I'll tell you where they learned a Nazi salute. Like the Kayans learned 'Waltzing Matilda' from Aussie paratroopers. Like the Ibans learned to cut their hair, throw away their beads, and sing 'Oh, Susanna' from moronic missionaries from West Memphis, Arkansas. The Kenyahs learned a Nazi salute from a Nazi. The Japanese were in Borneo during the war. Many of their skulls still decorate the *ruai* of longhouses. But there were no Germans there during the war."

"So this tribe—what are they, the Ubangis—?"

"The Kenyahs."

"The Kenyahs," said Ratso thoughtfully. "They learned

a Nazi salute from a real Nazi in the years after the war."

"That's correct, Watson."

"Interesting."

"Add to that that John Morgan would've never used the phrase 'anthropological land bridge,' as Dylan asserts that he did when Dylan told him the story of the white tiger and the Nazi salute. Morgan didn't know from anthropology. And he wouldn't go to the headwaters of the Ulu Ayer unless there was a damn good reason. And he had one. Find the guy who taught a gentle, primitive tribe, isolated for centuries from the outside world, the Nazi salute."

"So far, so good."

"In a manner of speaking. Now we know we have a Nazi in Borneo after the war. How do we determine his identity? We have the very telling gap-tooth business and the name Dr. Breitenbach. Add to that Stengal's remark to me that he was protecting 'the greatest genius the world has ever known.' "

"He was protecting Spinoza?"

"Not quite, Watson. Remember when Rambam bugged Dr. Bock's office? We were in the loft listening to my voice speaking under hypnosis, recounting the time, deep in the *ulu*, when I was getting a Kayan tattoo. Morgan was there, too, by the way, and probably not by accident. Anyway, remember the two small native boys I saw who appeared to be identical and had those startling blue eyes? They were twins, Ratso. *Twins.* What does that bring to mind?"

Ratso stared at me in mute horror. A large piece of walnut-apple-pecan cake that had been balancing rather precariously upon his fork fell off and made a three-coffee-bean landing in the middle of his glass of sambuca.

"In Auschwitz and in all of miscreation there was only one fiend whose specialty was experimenting upon twins. Though 'experimenting' is far too kind a word to use."

"So is 'fiend'," said Ratso.

I watched as his eyes took on an horrific understanding like a cold dawn over a parking lot that used to be the world.

"That's right, pal," I said. "The man Morgan was after was Dr. Josef Mengele."

"Too bad they don't serve German chocolate cake here," I said as the waiter brought Ratso a fresh sambuca. Ratso still hadn't said a word. He was just sitting there and slowly shaking his head.

"Abbie Hoffman," I continued, "once gave me a great recipe for German chocolate cake. The first step is, you occupy the kitchen."

Ratso chuckled a small chuckle, took a swallow of sambuca, and looked at me with a genuine fondness in his eyes.

"And it's just crazy enough to be true," he said. "You *are* amazing, Sherlock."

"You say that to all the guys."

"I guess something's being done about Mengele."

"Everything that's possible," I said, "which, I'm afraid, isn't much."

The waiter brought the check.

"Now tell me," said Ratso, "what the hell's the meaning of the grasshopper game?"

I chewed a coffee bean slowly and considered his question. I chased it down with the last of the sambuca. I looked at Ratso's gentle, intelligent eyes.

"I'd rather leave you, my dear Watson," I said, "with at least one mystery in your life."

Ratso got up abruptly, put on his coat, and walked to the door. At the door he turned to face me.

"I'd rather leave you, Sherlock," he said, "with the check."

Two days later, on a windy, rain-streaked Friday afternoon, I got a package in the mail from Wolf Nachman's office. I don't trust packages from lawyer's offices, so I opened it rather gingerly. Inside was Stengal's ceremonial dagger. The one that said *"Blut und Ehre."* Also inside was a bill from Nachman that was so monstrous it was going to require more blood and honor than I had to pay.

I gave the dagger to John Rapp that evening at a Thai restaurant on Eighth Avenue and Twenty-second Street that he claimed was the best in the city. As well as being an expert on matters of a Teutonic nature, he was also a prominent authority on Thai food. That's what we call eclectic.

John assured me that the SS dagger would be the centerpiece of his collection and he'd place it squarely between the World War I pointed hat, which is always better than a pointed head, and the 1944 Luftwaffe toilet-paper holder.

I did not tell Rapp that if you viewed his little collection from left to right, it would make, in many ways, a fairly accurate representation of the spiritual development of the German people.

There were a few more little problems that nagged at me that weekend, but after what I'd been through, they were nothing I couldn't deal with. The first was an irate phone call from McGovern, which I handled horizontally at 9:02 on Saturday morning.

"Who is this Peace Corps fuckhead who keeps calling me about some story I was supposed to write about John Morgan?"

"McGovern," I said rather groggily, "many thousands of young Americans served their country in the Peace Corps. I was only one of these idealistic young people. What makes you think I know anything about this matter?"

"Because I see a fine Jewish hand at work here," McGovern sputtered. "Last month you come over to my place to enlist my support in locating your old Peace Corps buddy John Morgan. I pitched in. I got you the obit from the Cleveland paper. I got you that coroner's report from my press contacts in New Jersey."

"Okay, McGovern, so I used your name in vain so I could get some information from the Peace Corps in Washington."

"That's the thanks I get for being your fucking leg man. Now the guy's hounding me and my editors every day to find out when the John Morgan story hits."

"You've got to admit," I said, "it'd make an interesting piece."

McGovern said something that was pretty unpleasant to hear at any hour of the day, and told me, in precise Irish terms, that it'd be to my advantage to call the guy off. I said I would.

Of course, I didn't. That was because I never really liked to talk to Norman Potts twice in the same twenty years. I figured either Potts would eventually wise up and stop harassing McGovern, or that sooner or later McGovern would cave and do a story on Morgan. He'd certainly covered more sordid stories than this. Where was his enterprising journalistic spirit? What would H. L. Mencken say? Probably not much, I thought. He'd been dead for thirty-two years.

I rolled over on my back, the cat curled up beside me, and we both went back to sleep.

It might've been eleven minutes later when Cleve called. If you think McGovern might be difficult to deal with on a Saturday morning, you should try talking to Cleve sometime.

"Kinkster!" Cleve shouted. "We're happenin', baby! 'The Kinky Experience' is happenin'!" It was brutal.

"Great," I said so unenthusiastically that only a crazy person could've misconstrued my lack of interest.

"And the *T-shirts*, dude, the *T-shirts!*"

"The T-shirts?" The only possible use I could think of for a T-shirt was to crush Cleve's larynx.

" 'The Kinky Experience' T-shirts! I've ordered ten thousand of them! My cousin Lissa is already selling them in the Lone Star gift shop. Lissa says they're the hottest-selling item she's ever had. We're committed, baby!"

"*You're* committed," I said, perhaps a little unkindly.

"Oh, that's no problem. My psychiatrists will let me go on the tour as part of a work-release therapy program. I only stay out for the duration of the tour. You're the one who signs me out."

"That's nice."

The conversation rattled along like this for a while on a very dangerous track, and finally, with Cleve and me shouting at the tops of our lungs and the cat bolting in terror for the living room, it jumped the trestle altogether. Cleve was shouting about his reputation being at stake, about contracts being in, and about the fact that if I didn't sign them he'd come over in person and see that I signed them. For my part, I kept repeating in loud, frazzled tones that "The Kinky Experience" was one experience that I never wanted to share with anyone, least of all Cleve.

Cleve ended the conversation on a mildly threatening note, alleging that if I didn't proceed with the tour he'd kill me, blow up the Lone Star Cafe, and assassinate the governor of Texas. He hung up with the threat still hanging in the air. It didn't sound too bad, actually. If he killed me, all my troubles would be over. If he blew up the Lone Star, we wouldn't get stuck for quite so many T-shirts. And if he assassinated the governor of Texas, who would notice the difference?

Later that afternoon Cleve's shrink at the hospital, a Dr. Numbnuts or something, called me to say that Cleve had had a little setback and wouldn't be eligible for the work-release therapy program after all for at least another four months. He reprimanded me rather strongly for encouraging Cleve with the idea in the first place, and wanted to know what he should do with the bill for the ten thousand T-shirts Cleve had ordered.

I told him.

"That," said Dr. Numbnuts, "is an extremely immature response, Mr. Friedman."

"That's good," I said. "I was afraid I was losing my touch."

One night the following week I was walking home from the Monkey's Paw alone in the gloom. Without Stengal around, the thought of skinheads hardly crossed my mind. Carmen was gone. The Left Coast kraut that Kent Perkins had uncovered was dead. Mengele, if he was still alive, had to be around seventy-seven years old, cowering somewhere in the jungles of Borneo. The case appeared to be fairly well wrapped up from this end. The only thing I still didn't know was the thing that had gotten me involved in the whole mess in the first place.

Where was John?

I drifted back to the time when I first thought of joining the Peace Corps. I'd told my friends at school that I was thinking of going, and if I went I'd be earning approximately eleven cents an hour. Most of them had said something like, How can you afford to go away for that long? When you come back, they'd said, we'll be in medical school. We'll be finishing law school. Where will you be? What will you have?

Now, many of them are working on their third careers and wrapping up their second divorces, and I'm a country singer turned amateur detective living in New York City with my cat. Things seem to have worked out pretty much the way they weren't intended, but as Joseph Heller says, "Nothing succeeds as planned."

I'd already felt the angel's wings brushing against my cowboy hat a few more times than I would've liked in the past month or so. Even without a family to look after, or a structured type of job to confine me, what else could I possibly do to find John Morgan? How much time could you afford to take out of your life in 1989 to search for a friend from the past?

There are still a few trees left in the city, and I happened to glance up into one of them, and suddenly I saw the monkeys. It was in the early days of my time in Borneo when I'd first met Morgan at a little marketplace in Long Lama. We'd gotten along right off the bat, had a few drinks together, wandered down a nearby hill, and watched the little Kayan kids with their haircuts that made them look like tadpoles, playing on the banks of the Baram River. Women were washing clothes in the river. It looked like a good idea, so I jumped in with all my clothes on. John jumped in too, but before he did, he took off the new shirt that he'd just bought and laid it on the branches of a nearby tree.

We were both swimming around in the middle of the river when I first saw the monkeys passing John's shirt back and forth up in the treetops. The kids on the shore were watching soberly, waiting to see what John would do. John yelled at the monkeys, "Hey! Give me back my shirt!" The monkeys started to get worried. They began passing the shirt around more frantically. Then they started tearing it up in little strips and passing the pieces of colored cloth back and forth in the bright sunlight. It was really something to see.

I don't know who started laughing first, but now that I think about it, it was probably John. Then all the kids started laughing. Then all the monkeys started laughing. Okay, chattering.

As I walked along the cold sidewalk in New York, even I had to smile. We were two young Americans, each weighing in at about 120 pounds, with, as I thought then, nothing heavy in our hearts, not a trouble in the world. It was a moment of pure joy. That was the way I would remember John.

I hadn't known what John was up to at that time, and when I considered it, I didn't really know one hell of a lot more about it now. That's why they invented "floating identities." I wasn't sure if John was dead or alive. I only knew he was in the world as long as I followed my heart and did what I wanted with my life.

Like Jesus, John Brown, or Joe Hill, Morgan had dealt largely in the casino of the spirit, and perhaps, like them, he'd bet a little too heavily on people. If I was ever going to find John Morgan, I'd pretty well decided, I was going to have to find him in myself.

I took a right on Vandam Street and walked briskly back in the direction of the loft.

There were a few more trees along the way, but I didn't see any monkeys.

69

I woke up one morning about three weeks later with a strange itch inside my heart. Everybody needs a vacation, they say. Of course, when your whole life's a vacation, it's sometimes hard to tell when's the best time to leave. This time I knew.

I called Winnie to see if she'd take care of feeding the cat and checking the answering machine while I was gone. In the background I could hear her putting her girls through a rather up-tempo version of "Gonna Wash that Man Right Out of My Hair." I tried not to take it personally.

Winnie wasn't overenthusiastic about my plan, but after a little bit of good-natured cajoling, she agreed.

"Thata girl," I told her.

"How would you know?" she asked.

I said I might be gone a little longer than expected, and I asked her if I should drop the key off at her place or if she'd rather just continue using the fire escape.

"Drop the key off, Bogie," she said.

I did.

Winnie took the key, along with a little kiss from me, and closed her door. I went back down to the loft.

I turned off the espresso machine, picked up my suitcase, and walked out the door.

I left the cat in charge.

70

It was a coffee-colored river. It seemed to flow out of a childhood storybook, peaceful and familiar, continue its sluggish way beneath the tropical sun, and then, at some point that you could never quite see, pick up force and become that opaque uncontrollable thing roaring in your ears, blinding your eyes, rushing relentlessly round the bends of understanding, beyond the banks of imagination.

ACKNOWLEDGMENTS

The author would like to thank the following Americans for their help: Dr. Tom Friedman, Dylan Ferrero, John Woodford Rapp, Jr., Alden Shuman, Hilda Pierce, Larry "Ratso" Sloman, Marcie Friedman, Tony Kisch, and Max Swafford; Esther "Lobster" Newberg at ICM; James Landis, Jane Meara, and Lori Ames at William Morrow; and Steve Rambam, technical adviser.

The author would also like to thank his five-year-old niece, Amanda, for the phrase "the grasshopper game."